5T

ONE SKY ABOVE US

THE ADVENTURES OF
YOUNG BUFFALO BILL

ONE SKY ABOVE US

BY E. CODY KIMMEL

ILLUSTRATED BY SCOTT SNOW

HarperCollinsPublishers

Grateful acknowledgment and thanks to Mark Bureman of the
Leavenworth County Historical Society

Library of Congress Cataloging-in-Publication Data
Kimmel, E. Cody.
    One sky above us / by E. Cody Kimmel ; illustrated by Scott
Snow.
        p.   cm.— (The adventures of young Buffalo Bill ; #2)
    Summary: Having settled on the Kansas frontier, young Bill Cody
and his family try to make a home for themselves, coexist with
their Kickapoo neighbors, and stand up as abolitionists in spite of
their neighbors' proslavery beliefs.
    ISBN 0-06-029119-2 — ISBN 0-06-029120-6 (lib. bdg.)
    1. Buffalo Bill, 1846–1917—Childhood and youth—Juvenile
fiction. [1. Buffalo Bill, 1846–1917—Childhood and youth—
Fiction. 2. Abolitionists—Fiction. 3. Frontier and pioneer life—
Kansas—Fiction. 4. Kansas—History—1854–1861—Fiction.]
I. Snow, Scott, ill. II. Title.
PZ7.K56475 On   2002   00-054344
[Fic]—dc21   CIP
                                                              AC

Typography by Andrea Vandergrift
1 2 3 4 5 6 7 8 9 10

First Edition

★ ★ ★ ★ ★

For my editor and friend Alix Reid,
who has Buffalo Bill's keen instinct and eye,
and who always asks where the horses are

★ ★ ★ ★ ★

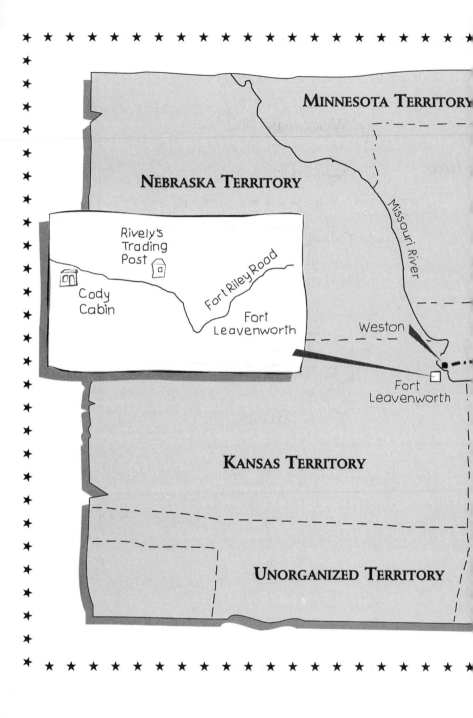

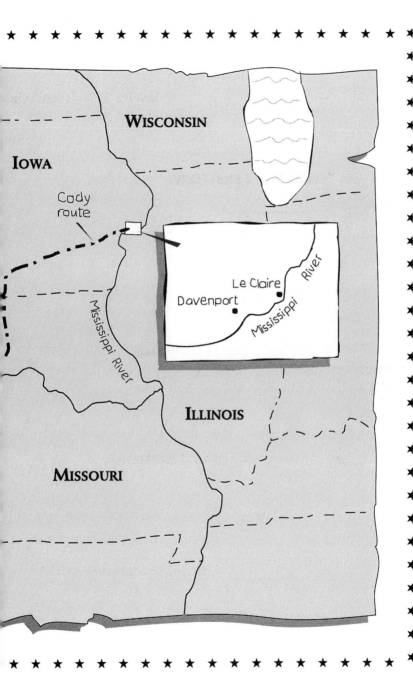

WISCONSIN

IOWA

Cody
route

ILLINOIS

MISSOURI

Mississippi River

Le Claire

Davenport

Mississippi River

CONTENTS

★ ★ ★ ★ ★

ONE SKY ABOVE US

CHAPTER ONE

PLANTING SEEDS

★　　★　　★

How the world had changed in just a few short months! Bill Cody ran a brush over Prince's back, and as he groomed his horse, he thought about what life had been like six months ago. The Codys had lived in Iowa then, and Bill's big brother, Sammy, had still been alive. Bill had never even heard of Kansas Territory.

He had been happy with the way things were, playing with his friend Joe Barnes on the banks of the Mississippi River and planning his life as a steamboat pilot. Then Sammy was killed in a riding accident, and before Bill knew it, Pa had packed the family up and set out to start a new life in Kansas Territory. Now Iowa seemed more like a story of someone else's life that Bill had heard time and again. It hardly seemed real. He was a Kansas boy now.

Bill never imagined there could be so much work for a body to do every single day. Each morning all the water the family would need had to be hauled in buckets from a nearby spring. What with cooking, washing, and cleaning, Bill quickly learned exactly how much water a family of eight actually needed. How he missed the well they'd had just outside their house in Iowa! Bill was also in charge of collecting wood for the fire. When he was done with that, he needed to feed and tend the horses and oxen, and the several hens Pa had bought for egg laying. Oftentimes he was sent off to lay traps so his family would have meat for supper.

Then there was all the building that still needed doing. Bill spent hours chopping and hauling wood from the creek for the split-rail fences. He marked more trees and helped Pa cut them down to provide lumber for their new barn. He cut shingles with

Pa's adze for the outhouse. Bill felt like he could never finish one chore without already being late to start another.

Today they needed to plow and harrow the cleared fields. It was almost July, and if they didn't plant the corn soon, they might miss their chance for a late-summer crop. It seemed everything had to be done right away, and it all took so much longer than Bill thought it ought to. When Pa had first told the family they would be moving to Kansas Territory, Bill had liked the idea of exploring and taming land that no settler before him had called home. It sounded like something his hero, Kit Carson, might have done. Bill had imagined it would be as dangerous and exciting an experience as any aspiring frontiersman might wish for. But the only things Bill had gotten out of it so far were sore muscles and a backache.

"Are you feeling neglected, Prince?" Bill murmured as he stroked his horse's neck. The animal's sleek brown coat looked like velvet in the early-morning sunlight. Prince gave a satisfied nicker and nudged Bill with his nose.

"I ain't forgot about those rides I promised we'd take. We'll get ourselves over to Fort Leavenworth yet, you'll see. But it ain't gonna be today, that's for certain. Right now the only thing I'm gonna be explorin' is the cornfield. I reckon I got a few more minutes for you, though. Get your coat nice and smooth with this brush. Feels good, don't it?"

Prince shifted his weight as Bill began brushing him more energetically, massaging the horse's rippling muscles with each stroke.

"You coming, son?" Bill heard Pa call.

Bill gave an exasperated sigh. Could a boy not have even five minutes to see to his own horse?

"Yes, Pa," Bill called back, doing his best to keep the irritation out of his voice. He put his face near Prince's and spoke to the horse in quiet, soothing tones.

"I'm sorry, Prince. Looks like your brushing is gonna have to wait. I know it ain't fair, but what can I do?"

He gave Prince a final pat and left his horse standing in the grassy pasture, hemmed in by the split-rail fence Bill and Pa had only just finished making the day before.

"I'll be back soon as I got a spare minute, I promise," Bill called. Prince gave a little whinny, which Bill took to be a sound of regret.

Bill jumped over the fence and started down the hill. He glanced back over his shoulder at the little barn, which was scarcely more than a few logs and a frame roof. It really had to be made more secure as soon as possible, Bill thought, to keep the wolves out, and the wind and rain off Prince's back. If only there were more time. Maybe if he stopped sleeping altogether, he might find enough hours in each day.

Bill couldn't help but feel sorry for himself as he trudged over to the field where Pa was waiting. It was barely past seven in the morning, but the sun already burned in the wide, cloudless sky. A slight breeze blew in from the west, but as Bill walked along, he could feel the sweat beading on his forehead. It was going to be a long, hot day, Bill thought, and all he had to look forward to was walking up and down the field as it was plowed and harrowed, with a thirty-pound bag of seed slung over his shoulder. Had Kit Carson ever endured such chores?

Bill joined Pa where he was standing on the border of the field, an eighth of a mile or so from their cabin.

"'Sa hot one all right," Pa said, removing his hat and fanning his face with it. "No lack of sunshine in Kansas Territory. Couple of good rains and we'll have ourselves a grand crop, Bill."

"We sure will, Pa," Bill agreed. Though it was hard for him get too enthusiastic about something like corn, Bill was still pleased when Pa talked to him like a fellow farmer. Since they'd moved to Kansas Territory, Pa had started treating Bill like an adult instead of a boy. This always made Bill twice as determined to act like a grown-up and never let Pa down. Even if it meant pretending to be happy about doing farmwork. Bill was, after all, the only other man in the family. He wanted Pa to know he could be relied on.

"Can't think what's keeping Doc," Pa said, scanning the horizon. "We need to get started soon if we want to make any progress on this cornfield. It's good land, though, and almost no trees or stones. Not like when I cleared Breckinridge's land back in Iowa. Digging out those tree stumps and hauling off those stones was some of the hardest work I ever done."

Bill had no memories of Pa's time on the Breckinridge land, when the Cody family had lived in the big stone house. He'd only been two or three at the time. But Sammy had remembered, and he used to tell Bill about the backbreaking labor of the job, and how Sammy himself had been such an indispensable helper. Knowing Sammy's dislike for hard work, Bill now wondered how much truth there had been to his older brother's claims.

Bill felt the hoofbeats before seeing anything. He looked up the hill, where Doc Hathaway was riding down to join them, waving his hat in greeting.

"Morning, Isaac, Bill," he called, stopping his horse and getting smoothly down from the saddle.

"Morning, Doc," Bill and Pa said at the same time.

"We were just beginning to wonder if a wolf got you," Pa added with a grin. Doc Hathaway smiled back, his sky-blue eyes twinkling from his lean face.

"Sorry to be tardy," Doc said. "Had to stop on over at Rively's trading post to pick up a few things."

Pa was already moving toward the plow and oxen. He had just bought the plow, which was made of steel and was specially built to cut right through the prairie sod. Pa would be in charge of the breaking plow, and Doc Hathaway was to follow behind him, his team of horses pulling the A-shaped harrow. The harrow would be dragged through the freshly plowed soil, and its iron teeth would rake and stir up the earth. Bill would come last, making little holes in the ground with a pointed stick and dropping in the seed corn. It would not be his most exciting hour.

Bill thought he might be a little more interested in things if Prince could be in the field working alongside him. Even if his horse was simply pulling the harrow, at least they would be doing something together. But he knew the animal was still too green for such work. By now he'd learned enough to know that hitching Prince alongside another horse and expecting him to drag a harrow might spoil the horse forever.

Up until last month Prince had been wild as the hills. Then Bill's cousin Horace Billings had come along and showed Bill how to tame Prince.

Bill took a moment to think wistfully of Horace. Horace had stayed with them a spell, teaching Bill all the boy could learn about horsemanship. Then he'd gone off to visit more family and, Bill was certain, to have exciting adventures. He was almost glad Horace wasn't around right now. Imagine having his horse-wrangling cousin to visit, and having to work the farm all day! No, better for Horace to keep away until the farm was settled, and Bill had something more interesting to show him.

Pa had already led the team of oxen to the field, and Doc Hathaway was in position behind him with the horse team and harrow.

"Ready, Bill?" Pa called, and Bill nodded, all thoughts of Horace instantly vanishing.

Pa shouted a command, and his team pulled ahead as he lifted the steel plow and strained forward. The oxen plodded in their steady way as Pa gripped the plow's handles, pushing it along like a wheelbarrow. The plow turned a strip of earth about two feet across, and the harrow churned it up to create a soft brown path. The air was slightly dusty, and thick with the rich smell of freshly cut grass and moist soil. The newly turned earth felt good under Bill's feet. He soon fell into an easy rhythm: the thunk of the pointed stick sinking evenly into the earth, the swift drop of the seed corn into the hole, and the swish as he smoothed dirt over the hole with his foot. Soon it was as easy as breathing—thunk, drop, swish. Thunk, drop, swish. Bill's whole world became the foot of freshly broken sod in front of him, the plunge of the stick, and the rustle of the seed bag. When Doc slowed up ahead, Bill looked up to see what the matter was.

There wasn't anything wrong. Pa had reached the end of the field and was guiding the oxen around to begin plowing the next row. Bill drew himself up and felt rather proud. That hadn't been so hard. His seeds were evenly spaced, and he knew he'd made each hole the right depth and covered it with just enough soil. It was a little boring, sure, but why shouldn't Bill find he was good at farmwork? He followed the path of the plow and harrow and headed around into the second row, settling quickly back into his rhythm. The second row gave way to the third, and fourth.

Maybe his talents were being wasted, dropping seeds. Bill figured one of his sisters, maybe Julia or Martha, could do it and free him up to work the plow. Pa could take the harrow. Really, why did Doc Hathaway need to come all the way over here when Pa had Bill? This very morning at breakfast, hadn't Pa said Bill was as strong as a young ox? When Pa paused at the next row to take his hat off and wipe his brow, Bill dropped his bag and sauntered over.

"Shall I take a spell at the plow, Pa?" he asked in a casual way. Pa stood with his hat in one hand and a surprised look on his face.

"Well, Bill," he said carefully, "it's heavier than it looks."

"Oh I reckon I've strength enough," Bill said. Doc Hathaway looked a little amused, inspiring Bill to add, "Pa himself says I'm strong as an ox."

"Can't hurt to let the boy try," Doc said, smiling at Pa as if the two men were sharing some private joke. Before even waiting for Pa's response, Bill trotted over to the plow, got his weight under the handles, and lifted as hard as he could.

"Now, hang on a moment, son," Pa began.

But he was doing it! He'd lifted the plow by himself! Feeling triumphant, Bill shouted a command to the ox team, and they began to lumber forward a little faster than Bill had anticipated. The plow's steel blade caught on a bit of turf, and it listed to one side. Bill tried to rebalance it, but the plow veered off to the side with a thud. The team continued to pull, dragging the overturned plow several feet through the last row before Pa was able to run in front of them and bring them to a halt.

Bill felt sick with embarrassment and shame. He'd gone ahead and picked up the plow without Pa's okay, and now he'd ruined part of the work they'd already done. He might also have damaged the plow itself. Red-faced, he walked over to Pa. What he'd done was awful, but it was better to face it straight out.

"I'm sorry, Pa," he said. Pa had every right to be furious with him, and he braced himself for an angry lecture and punishment.

"Well," Pa said after a long moment, "I reckon it does look a lot easier than it really is. Now you know. Dropping seed may not be the most exciting job in the world, Bill, but it's important, and you're good at it. Why don't we just do things like we were, and leave it at that."

Bill couldn't believe Pa wasn't going to punish him. He didn't push his luck. In a trice he'd picked up his bag of seed corn and stood ready to plant another row. Pa and Doc got back in position in the new row. With all thoughts of improving his lot gone from his mind, Bill got back to work and gave his full concentration to his job.

Row after row was plowed and planted, until Bill's neck ached from holding his head low to watch the earth and his hand grew raw where he gripped his stick. They had worked terribly hard and terribly long, but it would take a hundred rows, maybe two hundred, to complete the field. They couldn't be much more than halfway done. Bill's throat felt parched and fiery, his neck sunburned, and his feet swollen. Gnats swarmed around his head constantly, sometimes flying right into his eyes. Taking advantage of a pause as Pa turned the team, Bill leaned his head back and looked up into the ocean of blue sky. Far above was a soaring hawk, its wings outstretched as it glided on the wind. Bill felt a twinge of envy at the bird's freedom and thought how cool and quiet it must be so high in the sky.

"We're making fine headway, son," Pa called. "You're spacing them good and even. Keep it up."

"Thanks, Pa," Bill called back. He glanced at Doc Hathaway to make sure their neighbor had heard what Pa had said. He wanted to be sure Doc knew that, in spite of his bungling of the plow, he was still capable of good work. And they *were* making good headway. Surely even Kit Carson himself would feel some satisfaction working the land with his pa, creating farmland that would feed their family and fill their pockets for years to come. Bill followed Pa back around onto the next row, the hawk soaring overhead forgotten.

It was midday when Pa halted the team. Bill's sister Julia had come with a basket of lunch. Dropping his stick and seed bag, Bill walked eagerly toward Julia. He couldn't help but think that he must look very strong and manly, striding in from the fields for a noonday meal.

"Goodness, you look awful!" Julia exclaimed as he approached. "Have you been sick? Your face is all green."

"It isn't neither," Bill said with a slight scowl. "Just been working hard, is all."

"Well, don't you think I haven't," Julia retorted. "Do you know how many buckets of water I've hauled today? Not to mention how many dirty shirts I've scrubbed over the washboard, and let me tell you this, William Frederick Cody, yours are the worst of all!"

He'd practically forgotten it was laundry day. The sun would be setting by the time Ma and the girls had finished, and their hands would be raw and red all night. Had he not taken the time to visit Prince, Bill might have hauled several extra buckets of water to the house himself, saving Julia the trouble. He gave his sister a grateful look, feeling a sudden moment of appreciation for her. After all, she was about to feed him, and hunger and thirst were a powerful weapon against pride.

"I expect you're right," he said peaceably. "What d'ya got in there, Julia? I'm about to die of starvation."

Julia immediately began pulling food out of the basket as Pa and Doc Hathaway walked over.

"There's some corn pancakes and the last of the salt pork," Julia said. "And a surprise!"

"What surprise is that, darling?" Pa said, giving his daughter a kiss on the cheek. Julia reached into the basket and pulled out a little bucket covered with a cloth, which she handed to Pa. He drew the cloth aside and peered in.

"Plums!" he cried in delight. "However did you come by them?"

"Eliza Alice spotted them growing wild, and Ma let her take Turk out and pick some!"

Bill felt pleased that Turk, his beloved mastiff hound, was stepping so easily into his new role as protector and guardian. He missed having the faithful dog constantly at his heels, as he had been in Iowa. But here on their claim, Turk was playing a much more important role in the family. His keen eyes and protective instincts made him a formidable watchdog. Even Ma, who worried about practically everything, felt comfortable about the safety of her children when Turk was there to guard them.

Pa passed the bucket around, and Bill took a great, fat plum. It felt weighty and cool in his hand, and he was so desperate for a bite he didn't even bother to check it for worms. It practically exploded when he bit into it, the cool, sweet juice running down his chin. The fruit satisfied his hunger and thirst all at the same time, and he thought in all his life since and to follow, nothing would ever taste quite so sweet and be so refreshing.

As he ate his plum, Julia spread a blanket on the ground and set out their lunch. It took everything Bill had not to groan with relief as he sat down. He gave his favorite sister an appreciative smile as he reached for a corn pancake. These little domestic tasks did not come naturally to Julia. He didn't blame her. Even if he was only a seed dropper, he wouldn't have switched places with her for anything.

Pa and Doc Hathaway were speaking animatedly to each other about the crops—how long it might take for the fields to be ready and planted, how much sun and rain they'd need for healthy corn, whether the locusts had been pesky this year, and so forth.

Bill found himself wishing they'd talk forever, so that he could stay on the blanket with food and drink just a reach away. Now that his stomach was full, and the weight was off his feet, all he needed was a nice three-hour nap. Ideally by a campfire in the middle of the great plains, as Prince dozed nearby beneath an ocean of stars. There Bill would sleep long and peacefully, but not so deeply that a wolf or a horse thief might creep into his camp under cover of darkness. . . .

"You ready, son?" came Pa's voice. Bill's eyes snapped open, then squinted through the bright sunlight.

"Uh-huh," he mumbled, struggling to his feet. Before him the half-plowed field lay as an unhappy reminder of the work that remained. Bill picked up his stick and his bag of seed corn and followed Pa.

As he crawled into bed that night, Bill thought he'd never been so tired in his life. They'd finished the cornfield, but tomorrow would start all over again, this time plowing and harrowing under the second field to plant the wheat. There were generally many pleasant things for a boy to think about as he fell asleep—riding alongside the dragoons, or scouting out a new route to California, or outrunning a wild wolf pack. But this night Bill had no energy for imagination. As soon as his head hit the pillow, he was in a deep sleep, and he dreamed of nothing at all till Ma came to wake him in the morning.

CHAPTER TWO
NEWS

B ill dropped what he hoped would be the last armload of firewood onto the woodpile behind the cabin and gave Pa a questioning look. Tomorrow was Ma's baking day, and Bill knew she'd need to keep a fire burning straight through to supper time. Still, the pile looked big enough now, and Bill hoped there might be a few spare minutes for him to visit Prince. He'd scarcely had time to do more than feed his horse since they'd finished laying in the crops two days ago. Prince was certainly the smartest horse in all of Kansas Territory, but could he really understand that Bill was not neglecting him on purpose?

"I guess that'll about do it," Pa said. Bill's expression brightened.

★ 17 ★

"Well, then," Bill began.

"Leaves us enough time before supper to give your ma and the girls a hand in the kitchen."

"The kitchen?" Bill cried out, before he could stop himself.

"You have something else in mind?" Pa said, giving Bill a stern look.

"Not really," Bill said. "That is, I thought I might just check on Prince for a minute or two."

"I reckon you'll be more help to your ma," said Pa. He started walking toward the door, and Bill knew that subject was closed. Certain Pa wasn't looking, Bill made a face before following him into the cabin.

The cabin's door opened right into the kitchen, the cabin's main room, which smelled of frying ham and potatoes. Bill's stomach gave a little rumble as he glanced around at his sisters working at their various chores. His oldest sister, Martha, stood by Ma near the stove, where the ham sizzled hotly. Julia was setting the table, where Eliza Alice sat dutifully near the fireplace with her head bent over her mending. Other than Martha, Eliza Alice was the only child Bill knew who actually seemed to enjoy her chores. Martha had an excuse, he felt. At nineteen she was really a grown-up, and so just didn't know any better. But Eliza Alice was two years younger than Bill, and yet she seemed to have no desire to go outside or play pretend. She enjoyed nothing more than working at the endless piles of mending. Nellie, only four years old, on the other hand, was always begging to play, and at the moment she was trying to dress up Turk by tying a ribbon around his neck. Turk endured this patiently while the baby, Mary Hannah, seated on a quilt Ma had spread on the puncheon floor, watched with fascination.

Surely the girls had everything in hand, Bill thought in frustration. Couldn't Pa see that? But Pa's attention had been caught by a letter and a newspaper on the side table.

"Doc Hathaway brought them by while you were out wood hauling," Ma said. "He picked them up at Rively's trading post."

"A good fellow, Doc Hathaway," Pa said, pulling the rocking chair closer to the fireplace and taking a seat. "Let's see what we have here."

Well, that was that, Bill thought. Poor Prince was just going to have to wait again. Maybe after supper there would be time.

Julia helped Martha set out the platter of ham and the bowl of fried potatoes, along with the leftover bread from Ma's last baking day. Soon everyone was at the table, Eliza Alice helping Mary Hannah into the high chair Pa had made. Bill's stomach growled again as Pa gave the blessing.

No one spoke as Ma served the ham, filling Pa's plate and then the children's, one at a time. Although Bill and his sisters were allowed to talk at dinner, they had to wait until Pa started up a conversation. But tonight Pa seemed preoccupied with his letter.

"No bad news, I hope, Isaac?" Ma asked.

Pa shook his head. "Oh, no," he said. "The letter is from Elijah."

Pa's younger brother Elijah lived across the river in Weston, Missouri, where he was a successful and well-respected merchant and farmer. Bill wasn't sure he really liked stern Elijah. But Uncle Elijah had made a lot possible for Bill's family, helping Pa locate a good claim site and introducing him to officials at Fort Leavenworth to help secure their land. Uncle Elijah always said he knew what was best around these parts, and Bill guessed he was right. But it wasn't always easy being around somebody who was right so much of the time.

"Elijah's offered to help out with the barbecue," Pa said. "So I guess I'll go ahead with it."

"What barbecue, Pa?" Bill asked, forgetting that Pa was talking to Ma.

"I didn't want to say anything till I was sure," Pa replied, not seeming to mind Bill's talking out of turn. "I want to host a celebration here on the claim, for the Fourth of July, and invite all the locals. Indians, mostly. Kickapoo and their families. And Doc, of course, and the other settlers."

Now this was something indeed, Bill thought, sitting up straight.

"Really, Pa? Indians?" Bill asked excitedly.

Pa nodded, smiling at his son's enthusiasm. "There are plenty of Kickapoo living hereabout. I'm hoping to do some trading with them, now that our crops are settled."

"How many people do you suppose would come?" Ma asked.

"Few hundred, I expect," Pa replied. "Maybe more."

Ma said nothing, but the look on her face made Bill realize she had some misgivings.

"Don't worry, Mary, we'll manage. It'll be just like the barbecues we used to have back in Iowa, but bigger. And Elijah will help with the supplies we need. It'll be well worth the trouble to set ourselves up as friendly folk in these parts. I'm sure the Kickapoo will appreciate it."

"Won't the Indians scalp you, Pa?" Nellie asked, and Ma and Martha gasped simultaneously.

"Nellie! Where on earth did you hear of such a thing?" Ma asked.

"From Bi—" Nellie stopped herself. Bill looked down, but Pa just laughed.

"Not these Indians, Nellie-Belle. Kickapoo are

hardworking folk just like us. If we're good neighbors to them, I reckon they'll be good neighbors to us. That's why I want to have the barbecue."

"Any other news?" Ma asked.

"Family is fine," Pa said. "Elijah intends to pay us a visit in the next day or so, as soon as he can get away. Says he's volunteered me for some kind of committee, too. I don't quite know what to make of it."

"What sort of committee, Isaac?"

"He calls it a Vigilance Committee," Pa replied. "Something about surveying the claim sites. It all has to do with some meeting they had about putting down some guidelines for the territory. One of these new squatters' associations thought it up."

Bill caught Julia's eye across the table, and he made a face at her just to annoy her. She scowled back at him. Julia was unpredictable these days. There was a time not too long ago when she'd made almost as good a playmate as a boy. But she was different now. Half the time she tried to act all girlish like Martha, and lately she'd gotten so squeamish, it took almost no effort at all to get her to scream. She'd probably be scared of the Kickapoo, Bill thought scornfully. If only Sammy were here. Or Joe Barnes, his best friend back in Iowa. Then he'd have someone to get excited right along with him. He'd go tell Prince about the barbecue, after dinner. Prince, his only real friend in Kansas Territory.

"What is this squatters' association all about?" Ma asked. Mary Hannah's spoon dropped to the floor with a clatter, and Martha bent over to pick it up.

"It's about making sure everybody who stakes a claim in the territory gets a fair shake, I guess," Pa said. "And seeing to it that every settler has his own vote on the slavery issue."

Bill gave a quiet sigh. He had heard talk and more talk about the slavery issue, and he still didn't feel a whit closer to knowing what any of it meant. What he did know was that when Pa was just a boy, the government had passed a law saying that no lands north of a certain boundary would allow people to own slaves. The law was called the Missouri Compromise, and it was supposed to make sure that if those lands were settled and admitted to the Union, they would be free states.

But then a new law had been passed just this year, in 1854. The new law opened up some of the territories to settlers but said that the settlers would vote themselves whether or not they wanted to permit slavery. It seemed a simple thing, a vote for yes or no. It was beyond Bill entirely why the subject was discussed so frequently, and with such strong emotions, by just about every grown-up he saw.

On the trip west from Iowa, whenever the subject

came up, Pa always said that he had never owned and would never own a slave. He'd also say he was just a farmer, and that slavery politics didn't have anything to do with him. Then Uncle Elijah had flat out told him not to discuss his antislavery views with anyone. Pa hadn't been too happy about this, but the Codys began the grueling work of getting their claim settled, and the whole question of slavery had seemed little more than a distant rumble of thunder.

Pa was now telling Ma that the squatters' association had written down their aims in something called the Salt Creek Valley Resolutions. Bill halfheartedly tried to follow what Pa was saying for a minute or two. After all, Pa practically treated him like a grown-up now. He probably ought to know more about things like this. But as Pa explained to Ma what his committee was supposed to do, Bill's attention began to wander. He began to look around the kitchen, wondering if there was a bit of carrot or potato he might smuggle out to Prince. He could almost feel the velvety nudge of Prince's nose against his hand and the rough, whiskery feel of the horse's lips closing around the food.

Tonight the moon would be full. Wouldn't it be something to steal out of the cabin after everyone was asleep and take Prince for a moonlight ride! No one would know where they were going. It would be their secret, Bill and Prince's. They could run until morning, and when the sun rose, they could be back home, no one the wiser.

"Did you hear me, Bill?" Pa was saying. Bill blinked in surprise, then shook his head.

"No, sir, I didn't," he said. "I'm sorry."

"I asked you to hand me that newspaper from the table behind you."

Bill leaned over and picked up the newspaper. The main room was so small that their table of eight seemed to brush each wall in the room. He passed the paper to Eliza Alice, who was sitting next to him. She passed the paper to Ma, who gave it to Pa. He opened it up and thumbed through the pages.

"Yes, here it is, Mary. A whole article about this squatters' group. It gives rules of how settlers' claims are to be handled, and so forth. It all looks more or less—"

Pa fell suddenly silent and seemed frozen in concentration, the newspaper raised before him. The silence caught Bill's attention in a way that the conversation had not.

"What is it, Isaac?" Ma asked. It was a moment before Pa spoke. When he did, he was reading out loud from the paper.

"'Resolution number eight. That we recognize the institution of slavery as always existing in this Territory.'"

There was a brief silence.

"Well," Ma said. "You said before that this group meets at Rively's and that they're all proslavery men. So wouldn't that make sense?"

Bill hadn't been paying attention, so he wasn't sure what made sense and what didn't. Pa kept reading.

"'Resolution number nine. That we will afford protection to no abolitionists as settlers of Kansas Territory.'"

Now this was important, Bill knew. He tried to work out why. As a Northerner from Iowa who did not hold slaves, Pa was considered to be an abolitionist. And as near as he could remember, an abolitionist was anybody who was trying to get rid of slavery altogether. Protection to no abolitionist . . . protection from *what*? Could a person need protecting just for believing one thing over another?

"But surely that doesn't mean anything to us, Isaac," Ma said. "We know there aren't many Free-Soilers in these parts. Can't we just get along quietly, as Elijah said?"

"My name is on these resolutions, Mary," Pa said quietly.

Bill looked back and forth between his parents, growing alarmed. Now he wished he'd paid more attention when Pa was explaining all this. Why did he look so angry?

"Just on the surveying committee?" Ma asked.

Pa shook his head.

"My name is right here, Isaac Cody, member of the 'Vigilance Committee,' right in the middle of this resolution that says 'we' this and 'we' that. These are proslavery resolutions written by a proslavery group, and here my name is tacked on and printed up in the paper for the whole world to see!"

Pa's voice had grown louder, and the last word was almost shouted.

"But Isaac—" Ma began, but Pa interrupted her.

"I spent these last months doing what Elijah said, keeping my opinions to myself, and now I'm tossed in with a group making threats against me! And this is all Elijah's doing!"

Everyone had stopped eating. Nellie looked on the verge of tears, and even Mary Hannah was watching Pa, wide-eyed. Pa rarely lost his temper, and Bill knew how frightened his little sisters became when he did. After a moment Ma spoke.

"What do you mean to do, Isaac?" she asked quietly.

"I'll not be held up to be a proslavery man when I'm not. I intend to set this matter straight, and to blazes with whoever don't like it. Especially Elijah!"

Supper ended quickly after that. Nothing more was said about the Vigilance Committee, or Uncle

Elijah, or anything at all. Pa took little notice of Bill, barely nodding when Bill asked to go outside. Finally, a chance to visit the stable. But now Bill was upset, and he didn't enjoy the visit as much as he should have.

"Good boy, good old Prince," Bill murmured, rubbing the animal's neck vigorously. "I'm sorry I couldn't find a bit of carrot for you. Things got a little riled up all the sudden."

Prince stared at Bill with his soulful brown eyes. Bill leaned his head against the horse's neck, enjoying the soft warmth against his cheek and the good horse smell all around.

What exactly was Pa so angry about? Uncle Elijah had volunteered him to do something for a Vigilance Committee, and according to the newspaper, the group was made up of people who wanted Kansas Territory to become a slave state. Pa was against slavery, of course, and when the time came, he'd cast his vote to make Kansas a free state, and that would be that. Did belonging to some group or other really mean anything?

Bill supposed it must, if it had gotten Pa so riled. And he hated to see his pa upset. But there was nothing Bill could do to help the situation. He wasn't even old enough to vote in the election. There wasn't the slightest thing Bill could do to help make Kansas a free state, as Pa wanted. That was for other people, grown people, to sort out.

The most Bill could say about the whole subject was that it seemed to have ruined a nice supper and a promising conversation about an Independence Day barbecue.

CHAPTER THREE

THE GATHERING THUNDERHEADS

★   ★   ★

The corn shoots had pushed up through the soil, and the miniature plants stood in neat rows up and down the field, their leaves fluttering slightly in the breeze. Bill had to admit it gave him a feeling of accomplishment. Not much more than two weeks ago, each one of these plants was nothing but a tiny seed sitting in a bag. Now every one had become a living thing and eventually would provide food, and more seed, for his family.

Walking the length of the field, Bill examined the rows of shoots. If he squinted, they looked almost like columns of soldiers, dragoons dressed in green and marching in formation. The furrows of earth looked like little hills protecting the soldiers from the attacking enemy—weeds. The sight of those weeds brought Bill back to reality. His job for the day was to hoe the field. Every weed growing around the young corn shoots had to be done away with.

Bill stared at the all the corn rows that lay ahead, each one needing to be hoed. This *was* war, he thought suddenly. His little company of corn dragoons was under attack, and only General Cody could save them. Raising his hoe, Bill advanced on a cluster of weeds. He brought the hoe down sharply and chopped and sliced at them until they were gone. One successful attack. But the enemy were everywhere! Fearless, Bill advanced on the next cluster, his weapon before him. Yes, he was out-numbered, but he possessed superior strength and cunning.

There was another group. And another! With the swiftness and agility of a panther, fearless as a pack of wolves, Bill smote enemy after enemy, to the left, to the right, to the left again. He swung his weapon from side to side as he strode forward, the leafy menace falling to the ground before him. None stood a chance before him. General Cody at war was unstoppable. Nothing could slow him, nothing could lure him off the warpath. Even if he hadn't eaten anything, not even a morsel, in days. Weeks possibly . . .

Bill stopped with the hoe in midair. He was starving! It had to be time to eat soon. It seemed hours upon hours since breakfast. He looked off at the cabin. There just wasn't any way to tell what was going on inside, whether the table had been laid and the food set out. Still, Bill stood and stared as though he could will it to be time for lunch. Suddenly the front door of the cabin opened, and Martha came out. She saw Bill standing there in the fields and gave a wave, gesturing inside and patting her stomach. Bill dropped the hoe with a whoop and made for the cabin as fast as possible. Never was surrender so cheerful and swift.

Pa had been over at Doc Hathaway's claim all morning, helping him get his barn finished. Doc Hathaway was a good neighbor and one of the only Free-Soiler settlers around. Pa was glad to be of help. He came home to eat, bringing Doc along with him to enjoy some of Ma's fine cooking. Both men looked tired but cheerful, and everyone ate an enormous amount of Ma's leftover stew of wild turkey and potato. Bill wondered if they would talk about the committee Uncle Elijah had volunteered Pa for.

But they talked about the barn they were finishing instead.

"I know I'm repeating myself, but I can't thank you enough for sparing your husband today, Mary. Another hour or two of work and that barn'll be tight as a drum, and I couldn't have done it without Isaac," Doc said, taking a long sip of coffee.

"I'm just glad things are going so well," Ma replied. Bill snuck a look at her. He'd overheard her saying privately to Pa that she thought Doc was a pretty scatterbrained farmer, disorganized and always leaving things to the last minute. But Bill also knew that Ma genuinely liked Doc, with his open manner and pleasant, easygoing way. And no one was happier than Ma to have a doctor just a mile or so away. It was a luxury practically unheard of for a settler, and it gave her a good deal of comfort. For his part, Bill enjoyed the little gifts Doc usually brought along for the family. Today he'd brought a hunk of cheese somebody had traded him. Bill took another thick slice and ate it with a piece of bread. It filled his stomach in a heavy and satisfying way.

"We'd best hurry back and finish it up," Pa said. "I think we might be in for a change of weather."

Taking the cue, both men stood up. Pa stopped to give Ma a kiss.

"And you'd best press on with the hoeing, Bill,"

Pa said. "Looks like you're making real good progress. You were working fast as lightning when we rode up. Keep it up, and you may get it done before the rain turns the whole field to mud."

"I will, Pa," Bill said. He hadn't even noticed Pa and Doc riding in while he was working. The trail was on the other side of the cabin. He fervently hoped his war game hadn't looked too strange to the grown-ups.

After sticking his tongue out at Julia when Ma turned away, Bill followed Pa and Doc Hathaway outside. Pa and Doc were talking seriously to each other as they untied their horses, and Bill felt suddenly jealous. He couldn't hear what the two men were saying, but all the same he wished Pa was talking to him instead.

Glancing overhead, he saw what Pa meant by the change in weather. Where the blue sky had seemed endless just an hour before, heavy gray clouds were gathering, rolling in their direction.

By supper time it was upon them, the driving rains and crashing thunder of a real summer storm. Bill loved a good storm, and it was all he could do to stop from running outside and plunging right into it, to feel the cold needles of rain on his face. But it wasn't worth all the fuss Ma would kick up at the suggestion. Ma had eased up on him some since they got to Kansas, and she didn't worry about him so much, the way she had in Iowa after Sammy died. But letting him go out into a rainstorm—that she would not do. He'd have to settle for the satisfying noise the rain made as it hammered on the roof and the rumble of the thunder crashing across the sky.

Another great clap of thunder erupted. Eliza Alice, seated on a rug near the fireplace with her mending, gave a little whimper. Her pale-blue eyes looked huge. Nellie, on the other hand, clapped her little hands together with delight. She was stretched out on the other side of the fireplace, using Turk as a mattress. Ma and Martha sat at the kitchen table, stitching a pair of curtains. In Ma and Pa's bedroom, just off the kitchen, Mary Hannah was asleep in the trundle bed, deaf to the world.

Pa was examining several areas of the roof where some water was getting in. They had built the cabin as carefully as possible, but it was the weather itself that would ultimately show them where the wind and rain might get in. Bill silently added roof repairs to the growing list of chores that awaited him the next day. He hoped Prince wasn't getting dripped on out in the barn.

Pa hadn't put in glass windows yet, and there were still just strips of greased paper to keep the elements out. Feeling he needed just a peek or two,

Bill opened the door partway and peered into the stormy darkness. The air was filled with the rich smell of damp earth and the sound of the rain pummeling the earth. A fork of lightning pierced the sky, bringing a jarring second of daylight over the black landscape. Bill jumped back, and inside the cabin, Turk lifted his head and gave a low, long growl. It was not the lightning that had startled Bill but the momentary glimpse of something that looked like a dark, cloaked figure over by the barn. Turk leaped to his feet, spilling Nellie onto the floor, and shot over to Bill. Bill stared out at the place he thought he'd seen the shape. He could see nothing in the blackness, but when another bolt of lighting lit the sky, Bill jumped again. The figure was right in front of him now. Turk began to bark.

"Pa!" Bill called over his shoulder. Pa already knew from Turk's bark that a stranger was outside. He came quickly to the door and motioned for Bill to move behind him into the safety of the cabin.

Bill couldn't figure out why he felt so cautious, so wary. The settler's life was a sociable one, when there was any socializing to be had. Strangers as a rule were welcomed into the house and fed and lodged, with only friendly questions asked. Yet from the day Bill had first crossed the Missouri River into Kansas, he had felt a sense of danger, a need to be constantly on his guard.

Bill heard a few short words exchanged, then Pa suddenly turned and walked to the kitchen table. A wet hand reached in and pushed the door open wide. In the next moment, the man had entered the house, his soaked hat and clothes dripping onto the floor.

It was Uncle Elijah.

Pa said nothing, while Ma took Uncle Elijah over to the fireplace and helped him with his wet things. For some reason the kitchen no longer had the cozy, comfortable feeling it usually had. Bill found himself hoping that Pa did not actually mean to put things straight with his younger brother. He did not wish to see Pa get that angry again.

"I put my horse in your barn," Uncle Elijah said, holding his hands over the fire. In the dim orange-and-yellow light Uncle Elijah, with his tall, lean frame and thick, dark hair, looked a lot like Pa. "Wouldn't have set out at all if I knew it was going to storm so hard."

Pa didn't say anything, and the silence seemed very loud.

"You get my letter?" Uncle Elijah asked. Pa nodded but still said nothing.

His brother made an exasperated sound. "I just rode three miles from the ferry landing through a driving thunderstorm to get here. Does anyone have anything to say?"

"I got plenty to say," Pa said suddenly. He picked up the *St. Joseph Gazette* from the side table, where he'd left it folded open to the story about the Salt Creek Valley Resolutions. "But right now I'm more interested in what you got to say, about this here."

Uncle Elijah glanced at the article.

"The squatters' association, yes."

"You signed me up," Pa said, his eyes narrowing.

Ma stood up suddenly.

"Martha, the girls ought to be getting to bed," she said.

Martha nodded and took Eliza Alice by the hand. "Come on, Julia," she said. Julia threw Bill a look but followed her sister without question. No one said anything as the three girls climbed the ladder to their sleeping loft. Ma took a candle and disappeared into her bedroom with Nellie. No one said anything to, or about, Bill. It was as if he wasn't there at all. Normally he would bristle at being so invisible, but at the moment he welcomed it.

"You signed me up," Pa repeated at last.

Uncle Elijah gave his older brother an irritated look. "Are you talking about the Vigilance Committee? Isaac, that's about surveying land to record property lines. Have you gotten yourself into a state over that?"

They faced each other from opposite sides of the fireplace, the orange flames burning between them. Bill stood frozen, still by the front door.

"This squatters' association, these men, are pro-slavery fellows!" Pa retorted.

"That has nothing to do with you—"

"It has everything to do with me!" Pa cried. "You told me yourself, Elijah, to keep my head low on this slavery question. You told me not to air my Free-Soil views, to just keep quiet and make no trouble. Now my name is here in the newspaper, for everyone to see, in an association that says outright no Free-Soilers are welcome here! What am I gonna do when they find out I'm a Free-Soiler? What were you thinking, Elijah?"

"Of what's best for you and your family, just as I always do," said Elijah calmly. "You're a good man, Isaac, but you don't know how things work in these parts."

Bill loved his pa deeply, and though he found Elijah intimidating, he was still family. Hearing the heat rising in the two men's voices made Bill feel sick inside.

"Nobody knows how things work in these parts," Pa shot back. "This territory's been open less than two months. I know this ain't Iowa, but it ain't Missouri neither. It's new land with new ways and new problems that no one's seen before."

"But most folks in these parts are from Missouri," Elijah replied. "From Fort Leavenworth on up is mostly men from Weston and St. Joe who have crossed over to stake claims. And they aim to do things the same way they did them in Missouri. You don't understand, Isaac, you've never understood, the importance of staying in line."

"You're wrong, Elijah," Pa said sharply. "I listened to every word you said since I got here, and I took your advice. I ain't always liked it, and I ain't always agreed with it, but I went along with it. But now you've pushed me right into the middle of these men. I haven't called any attention to myself, but you've done it for me, Elijah."

Elijah shook his head in frustration.

"Isaac, you're blowing this whole thing out of proportion," he said. "This Vigilance Committee is concerned with only one thing, and that is the proper recording of the settlers' property claims. You're a good surveyor, Isaac, and you'll do the job well. By working on the committee, you'll earn yourself some respect, gain some standing in the community. That's the most important thing now."

"Haven't you read this?" Pa cried, seizing the newspaper from the table. "These men aim to have their way on the slavery issue, and they aren't going to stand for any man who doesn't agree with them. I may have been a bit blind before I got to Kansas, thinking I could just stake my claim and farm the land and keep my nose out of these political questions. But I've seen things going on in these parts, Elijah, and I've heard worse. Proslavers hunting down abolitionists, beating them, tarring and feathering men. You want these gangs coming after your family?"

Bill drew his breath in. Pa hadn't mentioned any beatings or tar-and-featherings to him.

Uncle Elijah sighed deeply and ran both his hands through his thick brown hair.

"All those things are happening, it's true. I don't condone it, but I also don't have any control over it. It's exactly what I'm trying to keep you out of. If anything, I've done you a service by linking you with the squatters' association men. If you do good work for them, they'll value you and respect you, and that makes it considerably less likely they'll allow anyone to harass you."

Pa thumped the newspaper. "'We will afford protection to no abolitionist,'" he quoted.

The same sentence that had set Pa off in the first place. Now, having heard Pa mention the acts of violence taking place against abolitionists, Bill could understand why Pa was so upset about the resolution. It would mean more violence against people who didn't want Kansas to be a slave state. People like Pa.

"I know what it says, Isaac," Elijah said impatiently. "You're just going to have to trust me."

"Why should I?" asked Pa sharply.

"Because I know these parts, and how things work, and I happen to be—" Elijah stopped himself suddenly, and Pa took a step closer to him. Bill felt things grow suddenly more tense.

"Because you happen to be what, brother?" Pa asked quickly. "Because you happen to be what?"

It was as if Uncle Elijah had suddenly crossed a line, though he hadn't even finished his sentence. Bill began nervously stroking Turk, who was sitting at his feet.

Uncle Elijah said nothing. Bill could see the muscles of his jaw clenching.

"Not going say it this time?" Pa asked. "That's all right. I heard it enough times before, Lord knows. I'll say it for you, Elijah. Because you happen to be smarter than me. Ain't that right?"

Uncle Elijah simply stared at his older brother. Bill could tell this was an argument the two had had many times before.

"Well, I've had enough," Pa said. "You sleep out the storm here, if you've a mind to. But then I want you out of my house. From here on I'm going to make my way in Kansas Territory with no help from you."

"Don't be ridiculous, Isaac," Uncle Elijah said.

"I'm glad to help you, and you need it."

"Do I then?" Pa cried, his eyes blazing.

"Oh, come on, now, brother, you know what I mean. Any settler in his right mind would welcome a bit of help. It's a rough business, starting a new life on the frontier. I've got some connections and some influence, and there isn't any reason in the world why you shouldn't benefit from what I've accomplished."

Bill knew his uncle was trying to smooth things over, but his heart sank at these words. Didn't Uncle Elijah realize how superior he sounded? This wasn't going to do anything to soothe Pa's anger. But what would they do without Uncle Elijah's help?

"That's very generous of you, Elijah," Pa said, in a dangerously pleasant tone. "What a shame all the other settlers have got to do without all your influence and your connections. I just can't see how any of them have a prayer of getting by without you."

"That's not how I meant it, Isaac."

There was a pause, and before he knew he was going to, Bill spoke.

"Pa, I think Uncle Elijah means well . . ." he began.

The two men snapped their heads around, surprised to hear another voice. Under their scrutiny Bill faltered.

"Don't speak out of turn, boy!" Pa barked.

Bill felt like he'd been slapped. Tears sprang into his eyes, and he clutched a fistful of Turk's fur in one hand. Pa had never spoken to him like that before. Never.

"The boy was only trying to help," Uncle Elijah said.

"I suppose you got advice on fathering a son to give me now?" Pa shook his head angrily. "No, Elijah, I've had enough. I don't want your advice anymore, or your brains, or your meddling. You cause more trouble than you fix. We'll be just fine on our own."

"You can at least let me help you with the barbecue. I said I would, after all."

"Leave it," Pa said angrily. "I'll do it myself, and I'll pay for it myself."

"Isaac, you don't have that kind of money. What will you do until the crops come in?"

"I'll find the money!" Pa retorted. "And there'll be no more talk about it. Stay here tonight, Elijah, but get you home to Weston tomorrow. I'll have no more of this."

"This is how you're going to treat me after all I've done? Your own brother?" Elijah said.

Pa's eyes blazed.

"I have no brother," he said harshly. Then, turning on his heel, he walked quickly into his bedroom and shut the door.

Bill took a deep, shaky breath. Uncle Elijah looked over at him.

"I'm sorry you had to hear all that, Bill," he said after a moment. "People say things in anger they don't mean."

Bill didn't say anything. It was one thing for Bill to feel Pa had done something wrong, but he bristled to hear his uncle suggest the same thing. Right now it seemed to Bill that the brothers were acting more like a pair of schoolboys than grown men. In any event, Uncle Elijah didn't seem to expect a response.

"I won't stay where I'm not wanted," he said, picking up his hat and moving to the front door. "I hope this blows over in a few days, when your pa has had a chance to cool down. But in the meantime I'll go." He put the hat on as Bill and Turk moved away from the door. "You know where to find me, though, Bill. If you need me, send word or come get me yourself. I'll not turn my back on this family. Remember that, will you?"

Bill nodded. Uncle Elijah looked at him for a moment, like he was seeing him for the first time. Then he turned and went out the door into the stormy night.

Silence descended on the little cabin as Bill tried to make sense of everything that had just happened. Uncle Elijah had made a mistake publicly linking Pa to a proslavery association, Bill was almost certain.

But he had done so with the aim of helping his family, however misguided he might have been. Pa seemed to have forgotten that. Would he really turn his back on Uncle Elijah? Had he meant it when he said he had no brother? For all the love and respect Bill carried in his heart for Pa, he could not understand how he of all people could say such a thing. Had Pa forgotten how terrible Bill had felt losing his own brother?

Sammy had been bossy, and pigheaded, and sometimes selfish. He'd been known to sit on Bill, to put a snake down his shirt, to toss him into the Mississippi River. But he would also lick any boy who dared mistreat his brother. He listened to Bill's secrets, and he kept them. For every time he had made Bill feel small, there was another time he'd made him feel ten feet tall. Even now it was sometimes impossible for Bill to imagine spending the rest of his life without his brother. But Bill had no choice. The minute that horse had reared and toppled backward onto Sammy, the matter had been decided forever.

But it was a different thing altogether to decide to do such a thing in anger, to choose to blot out a brother for good.

I shouldn't have let him leave, Bill thought suddenly. This is no night for traveling—Pa knew that. I should have gotten Uncle Elijah to stay. They might have talked things out in the morning.

Now it was too late. By morning Uncle Elijah would be at the landing, waiting for the ferry to cross the river that divided brother from brother.

CHAPTER FOUR
BUFFALO CHIPS

★   ★   ★

They were supposed to be gathering plums and blackberries, and fetching water from the spring. But the evening was sweet and cool, and the light of the sinking sun gave the landscape a magical glow. Bill had little trouble convincing Julia to wander with him a mile or so down the valley, near the place where hundreds of covered wagons were gathered at a campsite. It was said upward of a thousand folks had come into Kansas Territory in the last month, looking

to stake their claims and settle. Bill guessed that many of the wagons he and Julia could see would be heading into western Kansas, where the flat empty ocean of prairie would become their new home. Others were heading farther west still—maybe all the way to California itself, if they survived the trip across the continent.

"So many," Julia murmured. She and Bill were sitting on a grassy slope leading down to the valley where the covered wagons were gathered. "Why do you suppose they don't just stop here? The land can't get any prettier than this. Hills and valleys, trees and rocks to make fences. I hear out on the prairie there's no trees for hundreds of miles in every direction."

"It's true," Bill said thoughtfully. "But there's quite a few families settling here already. Doc Hathaway told Pa that some men from Weston are busy planning a town outside Fort Leavenworth. I guess some folks really want to strike out on their own, away from all that. And there's so much land to be had farther west, I suppose any man could have his pick."

Julia took a juicy bite from one of the plums. She spoke before swallowing the sweet mouthful.

"What I don't understand is how folks can live where there's no trees or rocks for a hundred miles,"

she said. "How do they make a fire? How do they build their houses, for that matter?"

"They dig 'em in the ground," Bill said, helping himself to a plum.

"They don't either," Julia said flatly.

"They do too!" Bill said, exasperated.

"You expect me to believe folks live in holes in the ground?" asked Julia, taking another bite of plum.

"Not exactly," Bill explained. "They call 'em dugouts. They find a little hill where the prairie's swelling up, and they dig into the side of it to make a kind of cave. Then they fix up a front wall and put in a chimney, and they got a house."

Julia looked doubtful.

"And that ain't all," Bill went on eagerly, always pleased to be the authority on any subject. "Some folks, if they got enough time and hands to help, make blocks out of the prairie sod, and build a whole house out of 'em like they were stones."

"A house made of dirt," Julia said, wrinkling up her nose. "Sounds dreadful."

"Sounds dreadful," Bill repeated, pitching his voice high and mimicking Julia's voice. "You sound just like Martha."

"I do not!" Julia cried indignantly. "I just meant that it sounded awfully dark."

"Keeps the wind and cold out in the winter," Bill said. "But Pa did say he heard stories about snakes coming down through the ceiling."

Julia gave a little shriek, to Bill's great satisfaction. In many ways Julia was as fearless as Bill himself, at least when Ma and Martha weren't looking. But when it came to snakes, she was near on hysterical.

"Yep," Bill continued, looking casually unconcerned. "Rattlers, mostly. They say there's more rattlers in Kansas than any other—"

A wet plum pit striking Bill squarely on the forehead silenced him.

"Well," he said, trying to look huffy as he wiped the plum juice off his face.

"What about fires?" Julia said, reaching for another plum. "How can you keep a fire going without wood?"

Bill, still rubbing his forehead, gave the grin of a boy who has been asked the one question he's longing to answer.

"They don't burn wood," he said.

"What do they burn?" Julia asked. Bill said nothing. "Sod?" she pressed. "Sod . . . logs, or something?"

"Nope," Bill said, taking the plum out of her hand and helping himself to a bite. "Not sod."

"Hay twists?"

Bill shook his head.

"Well, what then?" said Julia in an exasperated way.

"Buffalo chips," Bill replied.

"Buffalo chips? What are they?"

"Buffalo chips," Bill said. "Buffalo . . . chips."

Julia shook her head. "You're just not making any sense," she retorted.

"Chips that . . . come out of buffalo."

Julia's eyes narrowed. "What do you mean, come out? Come out of where?"

"Their tail ends, of course," Bill replied.

Julia choked. "Oh for heaven's sake," she cried. "Nellie might fall for that, but not me."

"Cross my heart," Bill said. "Ask Pa when we get home. The whole prairie is covered with buffalo chips from where they been grazing, and the sun dries 'em out. And families go out with buckets or wheelbarrows and collect 'em and bring 'em home, and they burn just as good as wood!"

Julia looked appalled and still more than a little suspicious.

Bill shrugged. "Don't believe me, then. You ask Pa. He'll tell you."

"I believe I may do just that," Julia said.

The two looked off in the direction of the setting sun for several moments.

"That was pretty awful, the other night," Julia said at last. Bill knew she meant the night Uncle Elijah had visited. He nodded.

"It was that," he said.

"You reckon Pa's still mad?" she asked.

"I don't know, Julia. He ain't said nothing at all to me about it. Except all the running around we're doing getting supplies for this barbecue, it's like it never happened at all."

"You think he was right?" Julia pressed.

Bill didn't reply right away. There wasn't another person in the world he could talk to about Pa, now that Sammy was gone. But this was Julia, his favorite sister. And he had a lot of things bottled up inside him he wouldn't mind airing out.

"I think he was right about Uncle Elijah making a mistake. But I think he was wrong, dead wrong, to react so powerful," Bill said. "Say what you will, and I'll agree with most of it, but Uncle Elijah's done a whole lot for us. I just don't see what good can come out of family turning on family."

"You don't think things will calm down after a spell?" Julia asked hopefully.

"Pa's about as mad as a man can get," replied Bill. "It's like he's been angry for years on end and it just all came out. You know how stubborn he is when he makes his mind up on a thing. I think it would take something pretty big to change his mind."

Julia looked worried.

"Oh, I expect things will come out all right in the end," Bill added hastily. "Somehow it will work out. And Uncle Elijah told me, before he left, that I should come to him if there's any need. *We* can still depend on him, Julia, even if Pa won't."

Julia nodded thoughtfully and looked out over the darkening landscape.

"Goodness, the sun's gone down!" she cried, suddenly. "And we haven't even fetched the water."

"And we've eaten half the plums we picked," Bill added ruefully.

"I wish we had a well," Julia said as they got up reluctantly. "I am so tired of hauling buckets of water every day!"

She and Bill picked up the baskets they'd used to collect the plums and blackberries. Bill cast one final glance over his shoulder at the sight of the covered wagons in the twilight. Tomorrow those wagons would head out west, into the unknown. Bill envied those pioneers, who still had adventures ahead of them. But he was a settler now, and his many responsibilities lay at home. And at the spring, collecting water for the next day.

Darkness seemed to come quickly once the sun had fully set. There was no moon at all, and but for the little pinpricks of flame made by campfires in the distance, the world seemed completely devoid of light. Bill began to walk faster, and Julia trotted to keep up with him.

"Look!" Julia said suddenly, pointing. Ahead, they could see a tiny yellow light where their cabin ought to be.

"Ma's put a lantern outside the window," Bill said, trying not to sound relieved. "As if we'd get lost," he added.

"Lost," Julia repeated, with a silly laugh.

"We should be coming up on the spring pretty soon, then," Bill said.

He could feel the beginning of a slight incline beneath his feet and could picture exactly where they were in spite of the dark. It was a talent he'd always had, to use his memory and instinct to find his way. Bill learned land quickly—by year's end he expected there wouldn't be an acre in Salt Creek Valley he wouldn't know by heart. He'd be able to cross one end of the valley to the other blindfolded, if need be. Bill didn't know where such a talent might get one in the world, but he was proud of it nonetheless.

"Just a few more yards," he said to Julia. As he spoke, there came the sound of an animal moving through the grass. Julia stiffened.

"What was that?" she whispered.

"Just keep walking," Bill replied.

"But what do you think it was?"

Bill didn't answer. He focused all his energy on listening, but he did not hear the noise again.

"Bill? You reckon there's panthers around here?"

"Probably," he replied airily. Privately, he knew what they had heard was much smaller than a panther, but he didn't mind giving Julia a bit of a scare.

Bill felt the temperature drop slightly and knew they had arrived at the spring.

"We're here, Julia," he said. "The buckets should be right around here somewhere—yep, here they are."

They put down their baskets of plums. Bill handed Julia one bucket and took another himself. His foot connected with something cold and smooth, and he reached down and felt it.

"There's a lantern here!" he said. "Ma must have left one. Now we'll have some light."

Bill handed Julia the lantern, with its little box of matches attached to the side. He knelt down and began to fill the first bucket with the cold, sweet spring water. After a moment a dim beam of yellow lantern light illuminated the spring. He heard Julia's quick intake of breath.

"Bill!"

He looked up and saw, beyond the stream by the brush, what it was that had startled his sister.

Eyes. Two pairs of yellow eyes, glimmering in the lantern light.

"Panthers?" whispered Julia, her voice shaking.

Wasn't that just like a girl, Bill thought. Anyone with two eyes in their head could see these animals were too small and low to the ground to be panthers. More than likely it was a couple of possums. But he couldn't resist.

"I'm not sure," Bill whispered. "But if they are panthers, then they've come to the stream looking to catch their dinner unawares."

Julia gave a little gasp. "Will they come after us?" she whispered.

"Only if they think they can beat us in a fair fight. Whatcha gotta do is scare 'em. Hold your arms out and howl loud as you can. We'll do it together—that'll scare 'em. Ready? On three—one, two, three!"

Julia stretched out her arms and howled at the top of her lungs. Bill, who had remained silent, collapsed with laughter. Realizing she'd been tricked, Julia swatted her brother in the head.

As Bill continued to shout with laughter, one of the pairs of eyes began to move, then another. The animals, whatever they were, seemed set on investigating the children. Julia, whose nerves were still on edge, gave a little squeal. Grabbing her basket, she pulled out a plum and hurled it in the direction of the eyes. There was a thud as the fruit hit its target.

"Julia, stop!" Bill cried.

But Julia, shrieking now, began hurling plums with both hands as hard as she could.

The animals turned their backs on the children, and the eyes were no longer visible. Bill was about to grab Julia's arm to drag her away when, all at once, a powerful and nauseating wave came over him. His eyes burned and watered furiously, and he began to gag and retch. He was practically flattened by the wall of smell toppling onto him. He coughed and spat on the ground, backing away.

Coughing and half blind, the children staggered away from the spring. Bill was so sickened by the skunk gas he'd breathed in, he could hardly walk, but he forced himself to put one foot in front of the other, dragging Julia along by the arm. His eyes burned too badly to open, so he stumbled forward, hoping instinct and luck would send them in the right direction. By the time he felt the familiar slope of hill underfoot, he was able to open his eyes just enough to glimpse their cabin ahead.

"Almost there," he croaked to his sister, putting his hands out in front of him. When they touched wood, he knew they had arrived. He felt along the wall for the door, and pushed it open. He was greeted with a chorus of dismayed shrieks.

"Oh, dreadful!" he heard Martha cry. "Take it away!"

"Bad smell!" Nellie's little voice piped in. "Bad!"

"What in the name of heaven . . ." Ma's voice trailed off. One look at her two children, coupled with the powerful smell coming off them, told all of the story she needed to hear.

"Don't come in," she said quickly.

Bill caught sight of Pa's face as he stood in the cabin behind Ma. His face was contorted slightly, more from his struggle to stop laughing than from the smell itself. This made Bill want to laugh himself, but he bit on his lower lip and the pain stopped the laugh from coming.

"We ought to just go straight to the spring and wash you, and bury those clothes," Ma said, leading the children away from the house.

"Not the spring," Bill said hoarsely. "That's where it happened. We'd best get down to the big creek."

"I'll take them down, Mary," Pa said from behind them. He couldn't quite hide his grin. "If you just fetch me some spare clothes and a lantern, I'll take care of the rest. And soap, a lot of soap."

Ma went back into the cabin, and Pa looked over his two children carefully.

"So," he said after a moment. "You went to pick blackberries and plums and fetch home some water. Looks to me like we got no blackberries, no plums, and no water. And the water we got in the spring ain't gonna be drinkable for a couple days. That about right?"

Bill nodded glumly.

"We did pick the fruit," he said, "though not as much as we should have. And we just walked down to take a quick look at the wagon trains in the valley, but it got dark before we knew it. Couldn't see much at all by the time we got to the spring. We were fetching the water when we ran into the skunks.

They . . . I guess we startled them, is all."

"It was me that riled them," Julia said, her voice shaking. "I threw as many plums as I could. . . ."

She burst into tears suddenly, and Bill understood that somehow this was more embarrassing, more upsetting, for her. And in spite of that, she hadn't told Pa about the panther joke. Bill couldn't help but feel this was better treatment than he deserved. If he hadn't teased her, maybe she wouldn't have gotten so scared and thrown plums at the skunks.

"I'm suh—sorry, Pa!" Julia wept.

"Oh, come now, daughter," Pa said gently. He moved to put his arm around Julia, then thought better of it. "No real harm done, is there? We can pick more plums, and we'll fetch our water from the creek for a couple days. And after a bath, or two, we'll get rid of the skunk smell."

All three of them knew it would take more than a bath or two. It would be days and days, even with all the soap in Kansas Territory, before their skin and hair stopped smelling of skunk.

Julia tried as hard as she could to control herself, but she just couldn't. Bill had never seen her cry this way, like Mary Hannah might.

"Come on now, Julia," Bill said, but this seemed to make her cry even harder. It embarrassed him, seeing her like this, and made him feel uncomfortable. Then he had an idea.

"Hey, Pa," he said. "While we're waiting for Ma, maybe you can clear up a little misunderstanding me and Julia had. Can you tell Julia what folks settling out on the Kansas prairie burn for fuel in their fires?"

Pa looked surprised at this change of subject, but he answered nonetheless.

"Why, you must mean buffalo chips, I guess. Buffalo chips are what they use."

Bill grinned at his sister, who had been momentarily surprised into stopping crying.

"Buffalo chips," Bill repeated with a mischievous smile. "Didn't I tell ya?"

Julia's face was still red and wet, but she gave a small smile nonetheless.

Ma came outside with the soap and spare clothes.

"You're looking a mite more cheerful, Julia," Ma said. "Feeling better, then?"

Julia nodded and started toward the creek behind Pa. Bill followed closely on her heels.

"Julia, I'm sorry," he whispered at her back. "Thanks for not telling on me." Julia turned around, paused, then socked her brother on the arm as hard as she could.

"Okay, then," he said, rubbing his arm.

She packed a pretty good punch. For a girl.

Chapter Five
BARBECUE

★　　★　　★

I t was a near miraculous morning—cool, dry, and swept with a magical breeze from the western prairie. Bill rose before dawn, as did the whole family, to continue their frantic preparations for the Fourth of July barbecue, which was just one short day away. If things hadn't happened the way they had, Uncle Elijah would be there with them now, lending his air of calm and capable authority to the proceedings. Bill found himself missing his uncle's presence, even with all its bossiness and superiority.

Bill was also a little worried about how much all of this was going to cost, especially now that Pa would be accepting no help from Uncle Elijah. Though his family had certainly never been rich, this was the first time in his life Bill had ever worried about money. Many of the supplies they needed were being bought on credit. They would owe a great deal when all was said and done, and their ability to repay rested completely on the success of their first crops. If something happened and the crops failed, where would they find the money?

Bill shooed those thoughts out of his mind. Worrying wasn't going to help anything. He couldn't let these grown-up matters ruin what might just be the most exciting day of his life. Pa had guessed that almost two hundred people would be coming to the Codys' homestead that day to join in the celebration, and most of them would be Indians.

Bill didn't know much about the Kickapoo tribe, whose reservation lay just to the west of the Codys' land. Pa had told him that their name meant "those who move around here and there." Though the tribe had clashed with settlers in the distant past, Bill had heard that here they lived peacefully with the whites. The homesteaders out on the western prairie sometimes came under threat from the Comanche and the Arapaho, but here in the eastern territory things were calm. Bill bet his family had far more to fear from proslavery Missourians than from any Indian tribe.

Bill saddled up Prince, rubbing the horse's neck as he finished. Finally, a chance to ride Prince! He wished all his chores involved Prince. They'd be so much more enjoyable that way. Bill was proud that Pa trusted him to ride to Rively's trading post by himself, though there really wasn't any choice. Ma needed more sugar for the lemonade, and extra salt pork, and Pa simply had too much to do to go himself.

Though the barbecue wasn't set to begin until tomorrow in the late afternoon, Bill was anxious to get to Rively's and back as soon as possible. Who knew but some Kickapoo might turn up a day early? Bill didn't want to miss a thing. He had never met a real Indian before, and he'd had his first glimpse of them only the month before at Fort Leavenworth, when he and Pa had arrived to stake their claim. Would they have braids and painted faces? Would they be fierce or mild? Would they even be able to communicate with the Codys?

They quickly reached Rively's. The trading post was the informal meeting place for many of the local settlers, and normally it was crowded with boisterous men. But now it was still very early in the morning, so there were just a few settlers collected outside. Bill was glad of the early hour, for he found these large groups of men intimidating and never quite knew how to behave around them. The last time Bill had come to Rively's without Pa, Horace Billings had been along. The way Bill remembered it, even the roughest-looking characters ended up giving Horace a wide berth. It had certainly felt good standing alongside such a man.

Bill tied Prince up outside the post and gave him a pat.

"I'll be back in a jiffy, boy," he said. Prince nudged Bill with his nose.

Bill nodded at the men standing outside and walked into the roughly built log structure, pausing inside to let his eyes adjust to the dark. The trading post was about the size of the Codys' cabin, with a dirt floor and a long counter running the length of the building. Dry goods and supplies were stacked on shelves, arranged in barrels, or simply laid out on the floor. Mr. Rively stood behind the counter, talking with three men. They all turned when Bill came in, and he recognized one of the men as Doc Hathaway. He did not know the other two.

"Morning," Bill said, hoping his voice didn't sound as squeaky as he thought it did.

"This here's Isaac Cody's boy," Mr. Rively said to

one of the men, who was very tall and almost painfully thin. "His pa'll be doing surveying for our Vigilance Committee. Morning, young Cody. What brings you out so early this day?"

"Got some Indians to feed," said the thin man. His stocky companion laughed, and Mr. Rively joined in.

"Getting some last-minute supplies for the barbecue?" Doc Hathaway asked with a smile, and Bill nodded. He was glad there was a friendly face in the room.

"Yes, sir," he said. "Some salt pork and sugar."

"I'm certainly looking forward to the feast," Doc Hathaway said.

"How much sugar you need, son?" Mr. Rively asked.

"A pound please," Bill replied. Mr. Rively took his sugar nippers and cut a portion off of the large sugar loaf. He placed it in a cloth bag and began to hammer the sugar to break it up into granules.

"What I don't understand," said the thin man, "is why anyone would go to such trouble to feed a bunch of Indians."

"Everyone's invited, Earl," said Doc Hathaway. "Including you and Jack here."

So Earl was the thin man and Jack was the stocky man.

"That's all right," Earl said, narrowing his eyes. "But it'll be mostly Indians, and I still don't understand why any man in his right mind would take it into his head to have 'em all to dinner."

Bill didn't like the way Earl was looking at him, and he bristled at the tone of his voice. It sounded like he was being disrespectful of Pa. Bill wanted to jump to Pa's defense, but he felt nervous and shy. He was relieved when Doc Hathaway spoke up in his pleasant, calm voice.

"Seems a pretty smart thing to do, the way I see it," he said. "These Kickapoo are going to be our neighbors, and they've been on this land for twenty or thirty years now. Seems we might be of some help to each other."

"I don't need their help," Earl said. "You need their help, Jack?"

"Reckon not," Jack said, rubbing a hand over his unshaven face.

"How 'bout you, Pierce?" Earl said. "You need Kickapoo help?"

Mr. Rively shrugged. "They do good trading."

Bill would have given anything to turn and leave. He didn't like anything about Earl and Jack, and he wasn't all that sure how he felt about Mr. Rively. But he hadn't gotten the salt pork yet, and he couldn't very well go home without it. At least Doc Hathaway was here to speak up where Bill didn't seem able.

Earl shook his head. "It don't make sense to me to be neighborly to these people, when we ought to be pulling together to run 'em off."

"Why should we run them off?" Doc Hathaway said.

"This is U.S. land now," Earl replied. "There's no place here for these savages."

"There's a lot of land," the doctor said. "Could be there's room for all of us."

Earl shook his head angrily. "We're here to farm the land, to use it the way God intended. These savages just wander about killing game and sinning and wasting valuable farm country. If these heathens won't accept our ways, they need to move off this land and let us work it as God wants."

Doc Hathaway gave a small smile, but to Bill's disappointment and, strangely, relief, he did not argue with Earl any further.

Mr. Rively handed Bill the sack of sugar. "What about it, young Bill, anything else?"

"Just the salt pork," Bill said. Earl glanced his way, then seemed to lose interest.

"A man could work up a thirst here, Rively," Earl said.

"Just a second," Rively replied, returning with several pounds of salt pork wrapped in paper. "You reckon this is enough?"

"Yes, thank you," Bill said.

"I'll just put it on your pa's account then," Mr. Rively said. "If he ain't good for it, I reckon Elijah is."

Bill didn't like the sound of that. What did Mr.

Rively know about Pa's and Uncle Elijah's affairs? What business was it of his, and why should he speak of it in front of strangers? At least Mr. Rively didn't know that Pa wasn't taking any more help from Elijah. One thing had stayed a secret, anyway.

But should Bill tell Mr. Rively that? He thought quickly. No, better not to. Better just to get out. Bill took his packages and walked outside as fast as he could without looking like he was running away. He put the things in Prince's saddlebag and untied him.

"Care for some company on the ride home?" a voice behind him asked.

It was Doc Hathaway. "Sure would," Bill said. Doc mounted his own horse as Bill climbed into Prince's saddle. They turned their horses toward the trail and walked along in silence.

"Who were those men?" Bill asked after a while.

"That was Earl Simpson and his cousin Jack. Got themselves a couple of claims down south of Fort Leavenworth."

"Why does Mr. Simpson hate the Indians?"

"Oh, any number of reasons," Doc Hathaway replied. "Most likely because that's what he hears other men say, and because he doesn't know anything about these Indians. And doesn't want to know."

"What do you know about them?" Bill asked.

"Enough to think that we can all get along, if we

put our minds to it," he replied. "These Kickapoo, the ones who live in these parts, followed a chief called Kennekuk for many years. He died one or two years back, but they're still sticking to his teachings."

"What were his teachings?"

"I don't know all that much about it, but from what I understand, Kennekuk realized way back early that if his people were going to stay together and get along in the world, they'd have to make peace with white men and learn to live with us. He came up with his own kind of religion that's half Indian and half Christian. And his people are forbidden to drink, or commit violence, or have more than one wife. They've learned to farm the land the way the settlers do, and I hear they work real hard and do well here in Kansas. They're decent, peaceable people. We're lucky to have them as neighbors. Some of the other tribes ain't done so well, and have whiskey troubles and so forth. Real rabble-rousers. The Kickapoo are straight and up front."

Bill was surprised to hear the Kickapoo were farmers. He'd always imagined that all Indians lived on the move, hunting for food and moving about at will.

"Do many folks want them driven off?" Bill asked.

The doctor nodded. "These tribes here have already been taken off their land a couple times.

They were promised land in Missouri, but some years back the government pressed them to sell up and move again. That's how they came here to Kansas. But now this land is opened to settlers, and I reckon most folks would just as soon move the Kickapoo west again."

Bill just couldn't understand how anyone could feel that way. He thought it sounded exciting to have Indians as neighbors. He didn't understand why people would want them to leave, just because they were Indians. Life certainly would be a lot more boring if everyone was the same.

"I wonder what will happen," Bill thought out loud as they rode along.

Doc Hathaway shrugged. "Doesn't really have much to do with us," he replied. "We're best staying out of it altogether."

Doc was a funny sort. He was as goodhearted a person as anyone would want to know—generous to a fault and always willing to help out. Bill was thankful to have him as a family friend and neighbor. But sometimes he wondered about Doc, wondered what he cared about and what was important to him. Like the Codys, he'd come all the way from back east to stake a claim here in Kansas Territory. But Pa had told Ma that Doc was about as half-hearted a farmer as he'd ever seen. Pa had seemed to feel that if he didn't keep after Doc to get his fields plowed and his crops in, he might not get to it at all.

And by his own admission, Doc seemed to spend more time hanging out at Rively's, talking with other men and picking up on the latest news, than anything else. And he did seem to be able to get along with just about anybody, though Bill knew for a fact that Doc Hathaway was not in favor of slavery. He thought about how easily Doc had chatted with Earl and Jack at the trading post. It had been clear enough to Bill that the two men were not good sorts. They looked like trouble, and Bill did not like the way they had spoken about Pa and the barbecue. Still, Doc Hathaway had stood there talking away with them and didn't seem especially bothered by anything they had to say, even if he had offered a different point of view.

They continued their ride in silence. Bill couldn't stop thinking about what Doc had said, about the Indians not really having anything to do with the settlers. He decided he did not agree. We're all just trying to make our way on the same land, Bill thought. The same land, the same sky above us, the same for Indians and settlers, Free-Soilers and pro-slavers alike. We have everything to do with each other.

CHAPTER SIX

INDEPENDENCE DAY

★　　★　　★

The Fourth of July had finally arrived, and Bill was so busy, he could barely pay it any mind. He had to haul four times the amount of wood and water the family usually needed. He had to help clean the cabin, a task Ma insisted be performed thoroughly although Bill didn't imagine any of the guests would actually be coming inside. And he had spent the better part of the morning preparing the cooking area by digging a large hole in the ground. He had tossed shovelful after shovelful of earth over his shoulder, until his arms had burned and his hands were raw and callused. When he could stand in the hole up to his waist, it was finally deep enough. Pa then fitted metal prongs inside it. They had bought a beautiful steer from a fellow who supplied meat to Fort Leavenworth, and Ma had been busy skinning and dressing it all morning. Then she stuffed the steer with strips of the salt pork Bill had gotten from Rively's. Julia and Martha had been in charge of sewing the hide of the steer to make a large bag.

Now that all these things had been done, Bill and Pa lifted the entire side of beef into the hide bag and carried the bag of meat outside to the cooking pit. Pa had started a small fire in the cooking pit to heat up the metal prongs. Bill and Pa carefully maneuvered the bag over the pit and began to lower it down. Bill was very careful not to lose his grip and cause the meat to break through the stitching. Much as he was looking forward to the barbecue, Bill really didn't want to be anywhere near the claim if the meat fell out of its bag and had to be cleaned all over again!

"Easy, Bill," Pa was saying. "That's good. Make sure it lands right in the center of the prongs so it heats even." The beef had to lie straight across the rows of prongs as if it were a mattress.

"Perfect," said Pa, and they let go of the hide bag at the same time. Bill straightened up, his arms trembling from the weight of the meat.

He heard the cabin door bang closed, and Julia came out with Mary Hannah on her hip and leading Nellie by the hand. She hurried toward them as fast as possible without looking unladylike.

"Now for the rocks," Pa added.

"Oh, good," said Julia. "My favorite part. You'll love this, Nellie. You're too little to remember the last barbecue."

"We're gonna put rocks all over our dinner, Nellie!" said Bill to his little sister, and Nellie clapped her hands in delight.

"Can I help?" she asked eagerly.

Ma, who had followed the girls out, smiled. "Exactly like you, Julia, when you were four. You'd never quiet down until Pa let you put a rock on the barbecue."

Bill was just being born when Julia was four years old, so he didn't share these memories of her, but he laughed out loud just the same at the thought. It sounded just like Julia.

"Get a rock then, Nellie, and let's get started," Pa said. "This beef's got a lot of cooking to do before sundown."

"Pick out a good one for her, Bill," Julia said.

"Oh, I had my eye on one for some time," Bill said, winking at Nellie. "It's this one right here."

He picked up one from the pile of smooth round

rocks that he and Julia had spent a morning collecting. Nellie eagerly took it in her hands, and Julia held the back of her dress to prevent her from getting too close to the edge of the cooking pit.

"Now put it right on top of the beef, real gentle like," Pa said. They all leaned forward to watch Nellie. Even Martha and Eliza Alice had come out of the cabin to watch. Every Cody child at one time or another, except for little Mary Hannah, had been allowed to put the very first rock into the barbecue. Bill could remember how excited he'd felt the first time he'd lowered a smooth, round stone into the cooking pit, while Pa held tight to the back of his britches.

Nellie's brow was knit with concentration, her lips pursed seriously, as she leaned down over the beef, the rock gripped tightly in her two hands. When she was satisfied that she was in just the right place, she let the rock drop. *Thud* went the rock on the meat.

"Hooray for Nellie!" Bill cried, clapping loudly. Everyone congratulated Nellie on a job well done. Nellie looked almost faint with pride.

"Okay, now," Pa said. "Time's a-wasting. Let's get this job finished so's I can get the hot coals on."

Everybody helped now, taking rocks from the pile and placing them in the pit around and over the steer.

Before long the entire steer was covered with the stones. Pa and Bill then lifted a set of iron rods, which had traveled with them all the way from Iowa and seen many barbecues already, and set them on top of the rocks. Now Pa was ready to place the coals, which he'd been heating over a separate fire, in the pit over the rocks. The coals would heat the rocks, which would cook the meat on top. The hot iron rods would cook the meat from below. Bill didn't know why the meat couldn't be put directly on the coals to cook, but Ma and Pa said the coal-heated rocks were the secret to their barbecue recipe, and for whatever reason, it seemed to work like a charm.

Pa and Bill put on the coals themselves. The girls' long skirts made it too dangerous for them to help. Bill well remembered the story of how, years ago, Martha's skirts had caught on fire when the wind had ruffled her petticoats against a burning coal. Luckily there'd been a creek close by and Martha had jumped right in. Since that time, handling hot coals had been work for those in britches only.

Bill's face burned with the heat from the coals, and his forehead was damp with sweat. Soon he and Pa had arranged all the coals in a thick layer over the stones, using a pair of heavy tongs. Now all that was left was for the meat to cook. It would be hours and hours before it was ready to eat, but there would be plenty to do during that time. Everyone had chores assigned to them, and Bill knew that in less than a minute they would all be running off in different directions, taking care of the cleaning, baking, fire tending, and whatever else still needed to be done.

But for one moment they all stood there together, around the barbecue, admiring their work and sniffing for the first faint whiff of cooking beef.

Look, Sammy, Bill said silently to his older brother. We're having a Cody barbecue, just like back in Iowa. And Sammy, you won't never guess who's coming to this one—Indians!

Chapter Seven

CHILDREN OF THE PROPHET

★ ★ ★

As the sun began to move down toward the horizon, they came. On foot, on ponies, and the smallest ones on cradleboards, the Kickapoo filed through the long grass and up the hill to the Codys' claim. One moment the land had seemed empty, and now it was full of Indians, upward of a hundred of them. Bill and his sisters stood in the cabin doorway as Pa went out to greet them, Ma hanging slightly back.

Bill wanted to rush right up, ask a thousand questions, and see every one of them close up. He wanted to touch their ponies and learn their names. But he knew well enough to wait. Pa was the host of this barbecue, and it was Pa the tribe was honoring with this visit. So though his legs were quivering to get moving, Bill patiently stood back as the Kickapoo chief, accompanied by a boy about Bill's age, approached Pa.

The chief spoke to Pa in Kickapoo, and Bill could hear the boy translating the chief's words into English. The chief's name was Elk Horn, the boy said, and some also called him Mecina. Elk Horn made a gesture, and the boy held out some things to Pa. Bill could see they were gifts. Some furs and hides, and what looked like a kind of carved stick. Bill made out one sentence clearly: "The Great Spirit welcomes you to our land."

Pa accepted the gifts with a smile and thanked Elk Horn, then turned and gestured toward Ma.

"My wife, Mary. And my children," Pa was saying, pointing to Bill and his sisters.

Elk Horn looked at each of them, and for a moment his gaze rested on Bill. The boy felt a little jump of excitement.

Elk Horn was of medium height, and his shining gray-black hair hung just below his ears. He wore a round, carved medallion at his neck. At first glance

Bill couldn't help feeling disappointed, because Elk Horn's clothing looked more or less like any settler's. Where were the buckskin leggings and breechcloth, or the woven headbands and feathers? Bill had been expecting someone a little more, well, Indian. Still, Elk Horn made an impression on Bill. The chief's face was broad and strong, and his dark eyes shone as he looked over the family.

Elk Horn began speaking again, and Bill heard the boy telling Pa about Elk Horn's wife, whose name Bill could not quite get. Bill followed the boy's gesture and saw the woman immediately. She looked about Elk Horn's age, with long glossy hair hanging down her back. She wore a dress fashioned from light-colored deerskin that went over her shoulders in straps, hung halfway down to her knees, and tied around her waist with a short sash. She wore a necklace of many strands of brightly painted beads, and beaded earrings hung from her ears. Bill looked at her face briefly but found her finely sculpted features and austere gaze rather intimidating. He quickly looked away.

The introductions seemed to be ending. Doc Hathaway had joined Pa over by Elk Horn, along with several other settlers whom Bill recognized from Rively's trading post. He was relieved to see that Earl and Jack were not among them. Looking around, Bill saw that Martha had already gotten back to work baking pies, taking Eliza Alice and Nellie with her. Bill didn't know how Martha could stand to get back to work when there were so many exciting people about, but then again, maybe Martha had seen lots of Indians before. She was a puzzle, that Martha. Bill remembered how Martha had once stood up in the middle of the dining room of a tavern to defend the reputation of Kit Carson, Bill's hero, whom she had once met. Bill had almost fallen out of his chair with shock. Martha was eleven years older than Bill. Her own ma had died when she was just a tiny girl, and she couldn't have been older than Nellie when Pa married Ma. So she'd had plenty of living before Bill came along, and he wouldn't be at all surprised to find out that some of it had involved Indians. But let Martha go and bake. There would be plenty of time to ask her questions later, and he had better things to do now.

Bill felt a slight pressure on his elbow, and turned to see a wide-eyed Julia standing beside him. He grinned.

"They're so . . . so beautiful!" Julia whispered. "But they look so serious."

Bill realized Julia was right. They did look serious, especially Elk Horn.

"Like they're at church or something," he whispered back, and Julia nodded. But there was also a strong sense of peaceful goodwill about them, Bill thought. They seemed so comfortable, somehow, in their own skins. Bill decided that he liked these Kickapoo.

The boy who had translated the conversation between Elk Horn and Pa had wandered toward the cabin, and his eyes fell on Bill. He was slightly built, but wiry and strong looking. He was dressed more or less like Bill, in a light-colored shirt and britches, but he wore moccasins on his feet instead of boots. They were probably almost the same age, Bill thought. The two boys stared at each other in an open, pleasant way. Then Bill made a gesture with his hands that meant "come on over." Without hesitation the boy came. They stood close together for a moment, still examining each other. Then Bill pointed to himself.

"Bill," he said, very slowly. "My name. Billllll." And he tapped himself on the chest for emphasis. "Jul-ee-a," he added, pointing to Julia. "Bill siss-terr."

The boy grinned.

"Nice to meet you, Bill and Julia. My name is Opkee."

Bill's face turned slightly red with embarrassment. Of course the boy spoke English well—otherwise he would not have been translator to the chief.

"Barbecue smells good. Or maybe," Opkee added with a mischievous smile, "I should say 'barbecue smell heap good.'"

Bill grinned back good-naturedly. "Sorry to be

so thick skulled," he said. "I should have realized you spoke English well. Where did you learn?"

"Kickapoo Mission, at first," replied Opkee. "The Honnells lived there, and the Hubbards. They teach the Kickapoo English and help with farming. It was harder for the older ones, but us little ones learned to speak it quickly."

Doc Hathaway had visited the mission, a two-story stone building on the government road connecting Fort Leavenworth with Fort Laramie.

"And we speak only English in school," Opkee continued. "Our teacher is named Miss Kooken. She came by herself from Pennsylvania just to teach Kickapoo boys and girls."

"She came out all alone?" asked Julia. She had felt too shy to speak until then, but Bill could tell she was intrigued by the idea of this lone schoolteacher.

Opkee nodded. "She lives at the mission. Right away she let some boys teach her to ride Indian ponies, and now she can do it almost as well as any Indian girl. She rides from village to village, visiting the children's families. Spending the night in their cabins. All the Kickapoo like Miss Kooken."

"Cabins?" Bill asked. "What about—I mean, don't you sleep in . . ."

"Log cabins mostly," Opkee said, looking like he was losing his patience a little. "Some still live the old way, in wickiups. Most build log cabins near their farmland. Just like you."

Bill tried to hide his disappointment. Here he was finally meeting real Indians, maybe even getting one for a friend, and they seemed just like everybody else! But Bill knew it wasn't true. These Kickapoo, this boy Opkee, they weren't like anyone he'd ever known, no matter where they lived or how they dressed. Bill wanted to know more about these people. He wanted to know everything.

"Is Elk Horn your pa?" Bill asked instead. Opkee shook his head but offered no further details. The conversation seemed to be faltering, so Bill tried changing the subject back to something Opkee had been enthusiastic about.

"We don't go to school yet," Bill said. "We've only been in Kansas Territory for two months. No school built yet, and that's fine with me. I don't much care for it."

"School is good," Opkee said. "Miss Kooken teaches us what we need to know to live with our white brothers."

Bill wondered exactly what one did need to know to live with his white brothers, but he figured this was another question for a time when he knew Opkee better. He was hoping he and the boy might become friends, and he didn't want to accidentally say the wrong thing and ruin his chances.

Julia shifted uncomfortably from one foot to another.

"I'd best get back to my chores," she said

unhappily. "Though I'd really rather stay here and talk to you two."

"It is early," Opkee said. "We will be here until long after the sun has set. But do not be late for your work, or Keotuk will come after you," he added, lowering his voice and making a mock stern face.

"Who is Keotuk?" asked Julia anxiously.

Opkee leaned forward and spoke in a loud whisper. "Tribal whipper," he said.

Julia gave a little shriek in spite of herself, which made Opkee chuckle. She looked questioningly at Bill, who merely shrugged. He was the last person to know whether Opkee was making fun or if there really was such a person as Keotuk.

"I'll find you later," Julia said. She turned and walked reluctantly toward the cabin.

"Good sister," Opkee said with an approving nod.

Bill agreed, but all he said was "She's fun to scare." Then, not wanting to talk about Julia anymore, he asked, "Is Keotuk real, Opkee?"

Opkee grinned and nodded his head.

"Keotuk is plenty real."

"Tribal whipper?" Bill asked.

"Yes. The tribal whipper is chosen at the council fire, to punish bad children. Our fathers picked Keotuk because he is a fair man, and gentle. Our fathers knew Keotuk would never punish the

children too harshly. When one of us is bad or dis-
obeys, Keotuk comes to us and *swish!*" Opkee
slapped his hand onto his knee, then opened his
mouth in a tight circle, as if he was about to howl in
pain.

"Did he ever whip you?" Bill asked. Opkee
nodded, and looked rather proud of himself.

The smell of cooking meat was thick in the air.
The sun had taken on an orange hue and looked suddenly lower in the sky. Folks had spread out over the
hillside. Some sat talking and singing. Bill saw Doc
Hathaway surrounded by a group of Kickapoo braves,
but he couldn't help noticing that most of the settlers were keeping to themselves.

Some of the women were doing their own cooking. Opkee and Bill walked through the grass and
stopped where several Indian girls were cooking on
a small fire of coals they had built.

"My sister, Neota," Opkee said, pointing at the
smaller of the two girls. "And Pawnee Annie."

The two girls looked up and smiled at Bill, then
got back to their cooking. Bill watched them shape
several large flat cakes out of ground corn flour mixed
with water. They placed the cakes directly on the
coals and cooked the cakes on both sides, then pulled
them off the coals and dipped them in water to rinse
off the ashes. Neota spread a little wild honey on one
of the cakes, broke it in two pieces, and handed

them to Bill and Opkee.

"Thank you," Bill said, and Neota smiled. He took a bite of the cake and exclaimed with pleasure. It was hot and light and sweet. Opkee wolfed down his cake in two bites, said something in his own language to the two girls, and gestured to Bill to follow him as he resumed walking.

"Your sister is a good cook," Bill said. "What was in the cakes?"

"Just ground corn and roots," Opkee said. Bill thought he could have eaten twenty more of them.

"Why is the other girl called Pawnee Annie?" asked Bill, enjoying the way he and Opkee were strolling along like old friends.

"She is from the Pawnee tribe. She got captured by the Iowa during a war some years ago. The Iowa women adopted her into their tribe, and she was taught at their mission. Then she came to our Kickapoo mission to help with the smaller children, and she's been living with us ever since."

"Are there lots of other tribes living with the Kickapoo?" Bill asked. Opkee shook his head.

"Mostly the Potawatomi. There are many of them living here with our tribe, and our families have lived together for years. They are really Kickapoo now—the Potawatomi among us were joined with our tribe in a great ceremony. This is a good thing. There are not so many Kickapoo left now. Many have gone to

Mexico to follow Chief Kishko. Every year some more travel there."

"Why do they leave?" Bill asked. They had reached a little flat area downhill from the cabin, and they sat down on the grass.

"Some believe we will never be allowed to stay here," said Opkee. "Kickapoo came to Kansas Territory before I was born, when our great father refused to let us stay on our lands."

Pa had said the Indians sometimes referred to the president as their great father.

"Where was that?" Bill asked.

"In Illinois," Opkee said. Bill knew Illinois well. Illinois had lain directly across the Mississippi River from his old home in Iowa.

"For many years Kennekuk helped our people remain on our lands. The white man kept insisting we move. We did as Kennekuk told us. We became peaceful people, and farmers. Our tribe refused to touch alcohol or to raise the tomahawk. But still the white people said they feared us and that we must make way for them. Finally Kennekuk realized that we would never be allowed to live peacefully on our own lands. So we came to Missouri, then to Kansas, to live on the land our great father set aside for the Kickapoo."

"And the Kickapoo are on the same land now?" Bill asked. Opkee shook his head.

"We lived and farmed quietly for a generation," said Opkee. "We had been told that here we would be alone, always, and free to live in our own way. But then the white men began to cross the Missouri River and hunt and live on our lands. We hoped that they would leave, but they did not. More and more came, building cabins and riding horses over our farmland. Kennekuk had prepared us. He had told us that the white man would again come into our lives, and it happened just as he said. Once again we were told we had to move, to make way for settlers and farmers. Much of our land was taken away from us again. And so we live on the little land that remains Kickapoo, some miles to the west." Opkee was silent for a moment before continuing. "When I was very small, our Kansas lands reached all the way to the Missouri River. But now the homes of the white people are there."

Including ours, Bill thought all of a sudden. He hadn't thought much about the fact that when the government had opened these lands up to settlers, they were taking the land from someone else. That Opkee and his people had been pushed west to make room for Bill and other settlers.

"I'm sorry," Bill said suddenly. Opkee looked a little surprised.

"You do not need to be sorry," he said. "You came as Kennekuk said you would. All was foretold to us many years ago." He spoke in a matter-of-fact way, but he also managed to sound a little superior. Opkee tilted his head back in the air and sniffed several times.

"Good barbecue."

"It's probably ready," Bill said. "Let's go up the hill where my pa is cooking the beef. I'll make sure you get a good piece."

The two boys scrambled up the hill, Opkee slowing every once in a while to greet someone.

The steer was finished, cooked to perfection. Bill noticed a little guiltily that Pa and Doc Hathaway had already pulled it out of the cooking pit, but they looked cheerful as he approached, and not inclined to scold. They were already cutting and serving the food to everyone standing close by. Pa had built a makeshift carving table and was carving juicy fat slices of beef. Though being so close to the barbecue made Bill and Opkee even hungrier, they both hung back. Elders, both settlers and Kickapoo, would be served before any of the children. Bill had the feeling this was a tradition shared by every kind of family in the world.

Ma had set up another table near where Pa and the doctor were slicing the beef. She and Martha had baked loaf after loaf of bread. She had brewed pots of coffee, and a big barrel behind her was filled to the brim with good, sweet lemonade. Bill could scarcely believe it. Nobody in these parts had lemons to sell, but Mr. Rively had a concentrated syrup called essence of lemon that made wonderful lemonade. He had arrived hauling a small block of ice, which they'd chopped up and mixed into the essence of lemon and sugar water. The result was mouthwatering. Some settlers stood milling around the lemonade barrel. Several of them had fixed little red-white-and-blue flags to their suspenders.

Ma had also made barbecue sauce, using wild plums that Eliza Alice had collected and some secret ingredients of her own.

Ma caught sight of Bill and Opkee watching the food with wide eyes. Smiling, she broke off a few pieces of bread and motioned them over.

"Oh, thank you, Ma!" Bill said, eagerly taking a bite of the fresh bread. He chewed and swallowed more quickly than he should have, he was so eager to introduce Ma to his new companion.

"Ma, this is Opkee," Bill said, as soon as most of the bread had gone down his throat. "Opkee, my ma. Mrs. Cody, that is."

"I heard you translating for your chief, Opkee," Ma told Opkee. "You speak beautifully."

Opkee shot Bill a quick grin, then looked back at Ma.

"Thank you, ma'am," he said. "We have a good schoolteacher this year."

Ma's eyes lit up, and Bill wished Opkee hadn't mentioned school. Ma looked like she'd suddenly remembered the whole concept of learning after a long time of forgetfulness.

"I do wish Bill was back in school," she said. "I expect it will be months before we can even find a teacher, let alone get a school built. Perhaps this schoolteacher of yours could take on a few extra pupils."

"Well, it's on the Kickapoo land," Bill said quickly. "So it's likely to be quite a distance. We'd all have to go on horseback. That would be all right for me, of course, but what about the girls?"

Ma gave Bill a look that said sometimes he was too clever for his own good, but she let the subject of the Kickapoo school drop.

"All the same," she added, giving Bill an affectionate look, "I do mean to talk to your pa about starting a school of our own. Now I'd best get back to work."

Bill and Opkee took up a strategic spot near the carving table, close enough to see how things were progressing, but not so close that Pa would feel like they were agitating to be fed.

"Elk Horn says this is a very important day for our great father," Opkee said as they waited.

"You mean because it's the Fourth of July?" Bill asked, and Opkee nodded.

"That's right," Bill said. "We always have big celebrations on this day. It kind of being the country's birthday and all."

"And you had a big long war after the first birthday," Opkee said, getting that slightly superior look on his face again. Bill couldn't exactly argue. How irritating that Opkee should know enough about the Revolution to bring it up!

"We didn't really have a choice," Bill said, slightly defensively. "We tried to work things out with the English and just had to become our own country when we couldn't."

Opkee looked thoughtful.

"Long war brings unhappiness to many people," he said.

"I guess it does that," Bill said. "But it's long since over and done with. I don't expect such a thing will happen again."

"Still," Opkee said, "I will ask the Great Spirit to keep our peace."

"I'll ask him too," Bill said.

The hours seemed to fly by, and Bill could think of no way to stop time passing so quickly. Barbecue had never tasted so good, and the air seemed sweeter than any Bill had ever breathed before. Even the song of the crickets sounded unusually pure and melodic.

The last of the beef was long since eaten. The coals had almost burned themselves out, and Bill and Opkee took turns shoveling dirt into the pit to smother the last embers. It was dark now, but Bill knew the most exciting thing was yet to come. Opkee had told him that some of the Kickapoo braves were going to drum and dance, as a thank-you to Pa for his hospitality. People were already beginning to gather in a large circle near the corn-field, where the corn Bill had planted was now knee high.

As Bill and Opkee walked downhill to join the circle, a deep, booming sound stopped them in their tracks. The noise seemed to shoot across the sky, and almost as soon it had faded, it was followed by another, and another. Opkee gave Bill a questioning look. For several moments Bill just looked back blankly. He couldn't imagine what was making such tremendous booms.

Then all at once he realized what it was.

"It's the cannons at Fort Leavenworth," he explained, pleased to have figured it out. "They're firing a salute."

Opkee looked confused.

"You celebrate a birthday by shooting?" he asked.

Bill shook his head vigorously.

"No, no," he said. "They're not shooting at anyone. It's the act of firing the cannons itself—we call it a salute. It's a way of honoring a person or thing." Opkee gave what Bill was beginning to think of as one of his "looks." "Well, how would you honor something?" Bill asked, once again feeling defensive.

"We would dance," said Opkee, as if there was no question that it was the more appropriate way.

The guns boomed several more times before falling silent. Maybe a dance was a better way to honor something, but Bill thought that the sound of the booming cannons was one of the most thrilling things he'd ever heard. Even after the reverberations stopped, his heart beat quickly with excitement.

The boys joined the tribal circle, where the dance was shortly to begin. Most of the people gathered there were Indians. Looking around at them, Bill was pleased to see that the braves who were getting ready to dance looked more like the Indians Bill had conjured up in his imagination for years, with striped paint on their faces and feathers adorning their hair.

In the center of the circle stood several drummers. Their drums were made of some kind of hide stretched over hoops and fastened down tightly. Elk Horn also stood in the center of the circle, holding a dried gourd that had something small and hard inside, which rattled when the chief shook it.

The drummers started, beating their drums with their knuckles, and Elk Horn shook his gourd rattle and began moving forward in a circle. The other dancers soon followed. They began to sing, repeating words that sounded to Bill like "hu-way hu-way" over and over again. Sometimes they swayed from side to side, and other times they seemed to slide smoothly and leap forward, first upright and then low to the ground.

The sound of the drumbeat started softly but then grew louder, then softer again, alternating in rhythm from very fast to very slow. Bill could feel the thunk of each drumbeat from the soles of his feet clear to the top of his head. The drumbeat made Bill want to dance himself. It took a great effort to stand still, but he made himself do it. This was a Kickapoo ceremonial dance. Bill intended to learn everything he could about the Kickapoo, but right now he knew next to nothing. He sure wasn't going to risk offending Opkee or anyone else by doing something wrong.

Across the circle, their faces illuminated by moon and lantern light, stood Ma and Pa, their arms around each other. Julia stood beside them, holding Nellie on her hip. Bill stared at Ma and Pa—they looked like two people he'd not seen before. He was certain he'd never seen them looking happier. Pa was tall and powerful, yet his face was full of peace and appreciation for the Kickapoos' dance. In the gentle light Ma looked ten years younger, her gaze eagerly following the dancers on their circular path. Every once in a while she and Pa would look at each other and their faces would break into long, lingering smiles. Bill felt a great rush of pride for his parents. Ma was strong and kind and pretty. Pa was accomplished, sensible, and fair. Who could go wrong in the world with such a ma and pa? Bill felt that as long as they lived and breathed, no harm would ever come to his family.

CHAPTER EIGHT
TROUBLE

Where had the weeks gone? It seemed to Bill that the sound of the Kickapoo drums still lingered in the air, yet the harvest was in and a slight chill had arrived in the air. The Codys had worked hard in the last seven weeks, and it showed. The barn was finished—weatherproofed and wolf safe. Their corn and wheat had been more abundant than they'd dared hope, and Pa had fetched a good price for it, clearing much of his debt with Rively. The squash and pumpkins they had planted between the corn rows were fat and healthy. And because there had not been too much rain, almost none of the potatoes had rotted. The hay Pa had contracted to sell to Fort Leavenworth was put up and drying nicely. Everything Pa had hoped for had come to pass.

The harvesting itself had been exhausting. The corn knives had to be sharpened on the grindstones. Pa had dulled the blades of the cradles harvesting the wheat some weeks earlier, and now they had to be sharpened too. The sharper the blades, the easier it would be for Bill to mow the hay and cut down the corn plants. After Bill and Pa had cut down all the corn plants, Julia and Eliza Alice bound together the stalks and ears and stacked them with the butt ends facing down in piles called shocks.

Bill had built the corncrib entirely by himself. The wooden structure looked like a little cabin up on stilts, with wide slats of wood where the walls should be and a deep sloping roof on top. The corn would be stored up high enough to keep it safe from scavenging animals, and the wide slats would let the corn air-dry while the roof kept the rain off. Pa told Bill there was nothing worse than harvesting a good crop of corn, then losing it all to mold because it had gotten wet. Bill felt Kit Carson himself could not have built a better corncrib.

Ma used the corn husks to make new stuffing for their mattresses. Martha wove some of the extra husks into mats for the floor and into collars for the horses. Once the corn kernels had been removed, the cobs were dried and used as fuel for the fire. Several of the best cobs were put away. When Ma had time, she would make them into dolls for Nellie and Eliza Alice.

Bill cut the pumpkins from their vines and rolled them into a pile in the unfinished barn. There would be pumpkin pie this winter. But Bill had no time to think about how good the pies would taste, because once the pumpkins had been collected, it was time to dig out the potatoes.

Each job seemed to create two more. But Bill cared less than usual. Yes, he was working twice as hard as ever, from dawn till sundown, and he barely had three minutes a day for Prince. But everywhere he looked there were rewards for all the work that had gone into the farm—real rewards that he could pull out of the earth, feel between his hands, and later savor in his mouth.

It was because things had been going so well that Pa had allowed Bill to ride along with him to Fort Leavenworth one day in September. Pa needed to finalize some details with the quartermaster about selling the hay. It would be only a week or two before it was dried and ready to be delivered to the fort. The money Pa would get for the hay would cover the rest of his debts and probably leave some over. Bill knew Pa was eager to be finished with his debts and to be getting by free and clear.

The ride east on Fort Riley Road had been

uneventful, but to Bill it was a rare treat to be away from the claim, riding Prince, and on a real excursion with Pa. He and Pa hadn't done anything like this since they'd come to scout out claim locations back in May. Bill felt very important riding alongside Pa, discussing the hay, and guessing how long it would be before it was dry enough to deliver to the fort. He and Pa might not have been scouting for a new route to the Great Salt Lake, but at least they were doing something new together.

Bill had wondered whether he should ask about Uncle Elijah. He hoped that Pa's temper had cooled by now and that enough time had gone by for the brothers to forget the unpleasant exchange. The rift really worried Bill, and he wanted to know what Pa was thinking. But it was so pleasant riding along the road with Pa, talking harvest and crop prices, Bill couldn't bear to spoil it. Maybe on the way back, he thought. That might be a better time.

Less than two hours after starting out from the claim at Salt Creek, Pa was in earnest discussion with the Fort Leavenworth quartermaster. Bill fetched some water for the horses and walked them over to a shady spot. He then found himself a comfortable position on the hillside, the Main Parade at his back, where the Missouri River spread out before him like a gift. Bill thought about all the people who had passed through the fort, from colonels and their companies of dragoons to trappers and mountain men hired to guide troops across the wild territories.

Pa had said the fort had been built around 1827, after the huge tract of land called the Louisiana Territory had been purchased from the French. Bill wondered that there was anything for the soldiers to do in those early years out on the frontier, but Pa told him that between making sure the fur traders crossing the country were protected and keeping the peace between various Indian tribes, there was plenty to keep them busy.

As the cool river breeze blew into his face, Bill closed his eyes and imagined what adventures he might have had at this great fort had he been born years earlier. He might have been along on Major Riley's first expedition to protect the trade caravans heading for Mexican territory with their goods. He could almost see the entourage, fifteen or twenty wagons strong, pulled through the ford of the Little Platte River by powerful, lumbering oxen. He could hear the war cries of the Indians protesting the presence of armed men on their lands. He could taste the frog and snake dinners that had sustained the men for so many weeks. He could envision the banquet enjoyed by the soldiers and their fellow enlisted men in the Mexican Army—a last indulgence before beginning the dangerous trip back to Fort Leavenworth.

Or he might have been a dragoon in General Kearney's Army of the West, setting out from Fort Leavenworth less than ten years ago to march into Texas and join in the Mexican War. Bill imagined Prince into the scene with him, gleaming brown and head held high, trotting proudly along to the sound of bugles, the rattling of swords, the fluttering of flags, and the clink of the cooking utensils striking each other as the supply train of over a thousand wagons set out toward the Great Plains. They would force their way through the rough country, marching nine hundred miles in less than two months, until they reached Santa Fe and raised the red, white, and blue there. The imaginary sight of the flag of stars and stripes fluttering in the hot southern wind almost brought tears to Bill's eyes. The very real sound of footsteps startled him out of his reverie, and he sat up quickly and looked around.

A young man stood looking down at him, a stern look on his neatly shaven face. He was wearing the blue uniform of the U.S. Dragoons, the cavalrymen who were often stationed at Fort Leavenworth. Bill had seen them practicing drills on horseback the very first day he'd arrived in Kansas Territory. He could see by the brass letter on the soldier's hat that he belonged to Company D. Bill realized his mouth was hanging open, and he closed it with a snap.

"Private Curtis, Company D, Second Dragoons reporting for duty, SIR!" the soldier barked suddenly, straightening to attention and stiffly saluting.

Startled, Bill leaped to his feet, looking wildly around for the officer the soldier was saluting. Was he not supposed to be sitting in this area? Had he broken some military rule? Would he now get Pa in trouble too?

But Bill couldn't see any other officer.

"Got ya, didn't I?" Private Curtis said, breaking into a grin. "That's a little trick we like to play on our friends when they're napping. Sneak right up behind them, and whoever is best at imitating the sergeant's voice shouts, 'Tennnnn-shunn!'"

Bill thought he ought to say something, but he honestly couldn't remember a single word.

"Nice day for a nap by the river," Private Curtis continued. "Caught sight of you as I was walking along the parade, and you reminded me of me, not too many years back. Eyes closed, face to the sky, mind who knows where. You from these parts?"

Bill nodded, still searching for his voice. A small miracle, he found it.

"My family's settling a few miles west of here, in Salt Creek Valley. Pa's meeting with the quarter-master, and he let me come along with him."

"And what's your name, son?" Private Curtis asked.

"Bill Cody, sir," he replied, and Private Curtis grinned again.

"Bill Cody, sir," he said. "Well you can call me

Sam, Bill Cody, sir. Pleased to meet you."

Bill felt a little twinge of surprise at the name, though it wasn't all that uncommon. He liked the fact that this young dragoon had the same name as Sammy.

"Are you—" Bill began. "Have you—" The question just wouldn't come out, probably because Bill wasn't quite sure what he wanted to ask first. Sam chuckled.

"I probably am, and I probably have. I joined up in the dragoons so I could see something of the world. My family comes from way back east in Massachusetts. I got tired of living in a little corner of the country, though it's the prettiest little corner you can imagine. I'm good on a horse and hearty as one, too, so this seemed like as good a place as any. My ma was none too pleased, though," he added a little sadly.

"I'd like to see the world too," Bill said. "Don't expect I ever will, though."

"Oh, now, don't say that," Sam said. "You want it enough, you'll find a way. You got to Kansas, didn't you?"

Bill nodded. "But there's not much going on in Salt Creek. It's pretty quiet. Only place anything ever seems to go on is here, and Rively's trading post I guess. Sometimes I do find myself wishing for a little excitement. We got our crops harvested and our place fairly finished. And back in July my pa had a big barbecue for the Kickapoo. That was something. But I don't see nothing coming now but winter, and not even that for some months."

"There's the election coming up in November," Sam said, rubbing the back of his neck thoughtfully. "Every day Free-Soilers and proslavers are coming to blows here and in Missouri. That's going to be one exciting election, young Bill, and remember that excitement ain't always the good kind."

"My pa's been trying to steer clear of all that," Bill said. "He's here to farm the land, not to do politics."

"Plenty of folks feel the same way," Sam said, "but I don't know of one of them that's gotten by without taking a side. Those who don't choose up make trouble with both sides, and that's twice as much trouble as anyone needs."

"So have you? Seen the world?" Bill asked, changing the subject to something more pleasant. Sam laughed.

"A bit of it, I suppose. A good bit. Haven't been out west yet, but I've seen some things around these parts that my own pa and ma might think I imagined."

"Like what?" said Bill. He was pleased when Sam sat down on the grass, leaning back and reclining on one elbow, and he sat down, too.

"Well, I saw a group down in Westport you just

wouldn't know what to make of. English fellow, some fancy title like baronet or something. Name of Sir George Gore, heard of him?"

Bill shook his head, feeling a pleasant tingle of anticipation for the story to come.

"Well, this fellow came over from England aiming to put together what he called a grand hunting company for the plains. And he did just that, and I happened to see them in Westport some months back, and I tell you, Bill Cody, you wouldn't have believed your eyes. Fifty greyhounds and staghounds he had in his camp, the most uppity dogs I ever saw. He had forty men, four six-mule wagons, two three-yoke ox wagons, and—I counted these myself, Bill—*twenty-one* French carts painted bright red, each of 'em taking two horses to pull. And one wagon was just for Sir George's guns alone, more than seventy-five rifles he had, and shotguns, too. And another wagon was loaded with all the things Sir George wouldn't go without, and would you believe it, Bill, he had a whole linen tent, an iron washstand, *and* a collapsing brass bed!"

Bill had to laugh out loud.

"Why would anyone drag along a brass bed on a hunting trip?" he asked.

Sam shrugged.

"I guess he does it because he can, Bill. Just because he can. So that was something to see, I tell you."

Bill thought Sam was probably right. There might not have been any marauding wolf packs or gun-toting bandits in the story, but it was a fine story all the same. Perhaps Bill should become a dragoon. Sure, he'd have to wait some years, and who knew what the soldiers might be up to by the time Bill was old enough to join them. But Sam looked so fit, and happy, and—well—impressive in his uniform. Excited by this new resolve, Bill cast a glance toward the fort, where he himself might well be stationed one day—and saw Pa striding toward him.

"That's my pa," Bill said, getting quickly to his feet. The pleased look on Pa's face told Bill that things had gone well with the quartermaster. Nevertheless, he knew Pa was in a hurry to get back home. No matter how safe Ma felt with Turk to protect her, Bill knew Pa did not like to leave her and the girls alone for one minute longer than he had to.

Sam had gotten to his feet and was introducing himself to Pa in his cheerful way.

"Pleased to meet you, Private Curtis," Pa said, shaking the young dragoon's hand.

"Your boy tells me you got some land just west of here," Sam said.

"That's right," Pa said. "A beautiful piece of property. Kansas has been a great blessing to us."

"Well, best of luck to you, Mr. Cody," Sam said.

Bill quickly checked Prince and Little Gray, adjusting the stirrups and tightening their girths for the ride home. In a trice Pa was in the saddle, and Sam held Prince's bridle while Bill mounted the horse. Giving Bill's horse a gentle pat on the rump, Sam stepped back as the two riders began to move away. Bill made sure his position in the saddle was perfect, his hands holding the reins evenly and just above Prince's mane, his heels down and his feet tucked under, so Sam would know he could ride well enough to be a dragoon.

"Mr. Cody?" Sam called suddenly. Pa turned to look at him as Little Gray walked forward slowly. Sam didn't say anything for a moment, just shook his head like he'd changed his mind or forgotten what he wanted to say. But as Bill brought Prince up even with Little Gray's shoulder, Sam called out to them again.

"Watch your back, Mr. Cody," he said. Pa nodded and waved again, and without waving back Sam turned and trudged off in the direction of the fort. Bill gave Prince his head, letting him stretch out his legs with slow, long strides.

"What did he mean, watch your back, Pa?" Bill asked.

"Just something one man says to another," Pa said easily. "Like wishing someone a safe journey, I expect. Things went well with the quartermaster."

Bill hesitated a moment, wishing Pa hadn't changed the subject quite so quickly. Then he chided himself for being anxious, as if he was Eliza Alice rather than Pa's only son.

"Did they?" Bill asked.

"We'll get a nice price for that hay, and more of the same next year with any luck. Just a few more weeks, Bill, and I'm going to feel we're really settled here. The hay will be sold, our debts paid, the barn finished. We've made good headway stocking up on meat for the winter, and Ma's been pickling and drying vegetables as fast as she can get to 'em. We're fortunate folk, Bill. Let's not forget that."

Bill loved to hear Pa sounding so enthusiastic. Moving to Kansas had been a gamble—he knew that. A lot depended on things beyond their control. The weather, for example. With too much rain, or none at all, their crops could be worthless. Or the weather might be perfect but the crops taken by locusts. Or, most frightening of all, cholera or some other terrible disease could strike the family. But none of these things had come to pass. Everything had worked in their favor. With such a head start, the Codys had every chance of becoming successful, and eventually prosperous, settlers.

After a time Rively's trading post came into view. Rively's was always a popular spot for the locals, but it seemed to Bill that today there were twice as many men there as usual. The men's voices combined to make a loud, angry, buzzing sound. As they drew closer, Bill could hear a mixture of shouting, laughter, and the occasional sound of breaking glass.

"Sounds a little over lively," Pa said. "Just keep your eyes on the road and ride on, Bill."

"Yes, Pa," Bill said. Pa sounded calm, but Bill could feel something electric and dangerous in the air, and he was sure Pa felt it, too.

"Isaac Cody!" a voice called from the crowd as they drew near. Another joined in, and another, shouting Pa's name in raspy tones. "Isaac Cody!"

There was no chance now that they could ride by quietly.

"Bill, keep to the road," Pa said, turning Little Gray toward the log structure where the men were congregating. "Just stay on your horse while I see to these men."

"Yes, Pa," Bill said.

"Promise me, son," Pa said urgently. "Give me your word you'll stay on your horse."

Bill's insides tightened. He'd never heard his Pa speak so seriously.

"I promise, Pa," Bill replied. Pa nodded briefly, then walked Little Gray over to the men.

"Morning," he called. "Me and my boy are just on our way home, or we'd stop with you a spell."

"You ain't too sociable, Isaac Cody," called one of the men, stepping forward. Bill recognized him as

Earl, the man he'd met at the trading post the day before the Fourth of July. "Seems you ain't never got time to say nothin'."

"Got a lot to do on my claim," Pa said in a pleasant voice. "I'm sure you all know how that goes."

Pa made a move to turn Little Gray back in Bill's direction, but another man took hold of the bridle.

"Charlie Dunn's got him now!" a voice called. Charlie Dunn held tight to the bridle.

"Been waitin' all week for this abolition cuss to come by," Charlie Dunn growled, and some of the men laughed.

Bill's heart began to beat faster. How many men were there in all? Forty? Fifty? Some of the faces were familiar. Bill thought he spotted Jack somewhere. But many of the men he'd never seen before at all.

"Now, we don't know what he is, Charlie—he ain't never said," Earl said, grinning as he looked back and forth from Pa to Charlie.

"Well, it's time we knew whar he stands!" Charlie Dunn shouted, and the men circling around Pa shouted in agreement.

"Tha's right, Cody. We gonna know where you stand!" voices shouted. "Right now!"

Bill sat, frozen, watching from the saddle, almost sick with fear. This crowd looked angrier and uglier than any Bill had ever seen, and he felt completely powerless. He was terrified some harm might come to Pa, and to his disgust he also found himself worrying that the men might suddenly approach him as well.

Several hands reached out of the crowd and pulled Pa roughly from his saddle. The crowd parted slightly, opening a path to an overturned crate set up on Rively's porch.

"No more cowardice," Charlie Dunn yelled. "He's let his brother Elijah do all the talking, but he ain't ever said himself where he stands, not one time! Let the hypocrite speak now! I ain't lettin' no man survey my lands unless he's man enough to look into my eyes and tell me he ain't no cussed abolitionist!"

"Now!" shouted Earl, and many men joined in. "Now, now! Tell us where you stand, Cody, out with it!"

Bill felt blind with panic. Pa couldn't tell them the truth—he mustn't. He did realize that, didn't he? It was a shameful thing to wish for Pa to lie to the men. But Bill wished for it with all his heart.

Pa was now standing on the box, facing the unruly crowd. He looked pale but composed. He did not look at Bill. Raising one hand, he indicated he was ready to speak. The crowd fell relatively silent, the quiet punctuated by occasional hisses and catcalls.

"Very well, then, gentlemen," Pa said. "Though I am not of a mind to make speeches, I am also not ashamed of my views. When my brother volunteered me for the Vigilance Committee, he did so without my knowledge or approval. I am in all ways entirely opposed to slavery and its extension to this territory. It is an institution—"

Pa's next words were drowned out by a chorus of shouted curses and boos. The men were not interested in Pa's reasons. He had given them the only information they wanted. Isaac Cody, settler of Salt Creek Valley, was a Free-Soiler.

"Hang the black abolitionist!" someone shouted.

"Shoot him!" yelled another.

Bill's heart gave a great leap of fear, but still he did not move. He had promised Pa, given his word. Besides, what could he do? Whatever his imagination might contain, in reality he was no Kit Carson, no dragoon. He was only a boy against a crowd of angry men. There was nothing, absolutely nothing, he could do but wait. Why hadn't Pa simply said something to calm the men? How could he have gone ahead and said the one thing that was going to rile the mob further? Bill experienced a momentary urge to turn Prince around and gallop away from the men, from Pa, from whatever was about to happen. His own fleeting cowardice sickened him.

Pa stood still on the platform. The shouting and cursing began to grow a little less forceful, and just as Bill began hoping the men would simply lose interest in Pa, he saw Charlie Dunn move behind the box, a glint of steel in his hand.

"Pa!" Bill shouted with all his might. "Pa! Look behind you! Look behind you!"

Bill yelled so loudly, he felt his lungs might explode, but his warning was entirely swallowed up by the sounds of the mob. He knew he had to move, no matter what Pa had said. He'd barely swung his leg over the saddle when he saw Charlie Dunn step up onto the box behind Pa, making a quick movement with his right arm.

It might have been a neighborly pat on the back, a friendly swat, but for the fact that Pa was sinking to his knees at the feet of Charlie Dunn, who was holding his knife in the air, the blade gleaming with blood.

CHAPTER NINE
REFUGE

★   ★   ★

His hands trembling, Bill tied Prince's reins to a nearby fence post. Then he headed through the mob, pushing his way blindly toward the place Pa had fallen. The crowd pulled back from him as he moved forward, and the shouting had stopped. The men were looking from one to the other, as if trying to sort out exactly how this had happened.

Pa was still slumped where he had fallen, his eyes open, his face deathly pale. Mr. Rively was kneeling next to Pa, pressing something onto his back. Bill

noted with relief that Charlie Dunn was nowhere to be seen.

"Pa," Bill said, trying to keep the fear from his voice. "Pa?"

Pa's breathing was strangely labored. He tried to speak but wasn't able to get his breath.

"Easy, Isaac," Rively said. "Let's get you inside." He glanced up at Bill.

"This is none of my doing, Bill Cody," he said. "If I'da known these men intended your father real harm, I'd have warned him off."

Bill nodded quickly. Under normal circumstances he might consider it quite flattering to be spoken to this way, as if he was an adult. It seemed to Bill these things were happening to another boy. And though he also wasn't so sure Mr. Rively was as innocent as he claimed, right now he needed the man's help.

"I'll help you get him up," Bill said, putting one of Pa's arms around his own shoulder.

"On three," said Mr. Rively. They stood up at Mr. Rively's count, pulling Pa to his feet as gently as possible. It was only a few steps into the trading post. The weight was almost more than Bill could bear. Because of the great difference in their heights, Pa listed heavily to one side. Many of the men had hastily departed the scene, but there were still twenty or so standing around. None of them tried to help.

Bill didn't know how he did it, except that he had to. Just when he thought he couldn't take another step, Pa was inside and lowered gently to the floor. Bill knelt at his side as Mr. Rively closed and locked the door behind them.

"We'll be all right here," Mr. Rively said. "None of them ruffians will try to break in while I'm here. But we're gonna need some help. This here wound looks bad."

Bill looked anxiously into Pa's face. It was completely drained of color, and his eyes were closed now.

"Doc Hathaway," Bill said hurriedly. "He's a good friend to Pa. I'd best fetch him."

"Now that may not be safe, Bill," Mr. Rively said. "Those ruffians may not have gone far, and Charlie Dunn is still about somewhere. Most of these fellas are all right when they're sober, but they're awful riled now, and none more than Charlie Dunn. If he went after your father, he might just as easy go after you."

Bill had certainly not forgotten how frightening it had been to watch that angry crowd. But he felt braver now. It had been hard to feel brave when he was powerless, but now there was something he could do to help Pa.

"Dunn can't catch me," he said, getting to his feet. "I got the fastest horse in the territory, and I know the land better'n anybody. You said yourself no one'll try to get in here while you're inside. If you'll stay with Pa, I'm going for Doc."

Mr. Rively nodded, looking relieved not to be in charge. Bill was almost to the door when he added, "Best hurry, Bill."

No boy had ever moved faster.

Prince was waiting quietly where he'd been tied by the road. The men still standing around the porch watched the boy dash to his horse, but no one made a move to stop him. Bill was in the saddle in a flash, urging Prince forward. The horse took to the road like lightning.

Doc Hathaway's claim was just west of the Codys', perhaps two miles from the trading post. Bill steered Prince off the road and onto the grass, pointing him in a straight line toward the Hathaway cabin. It would be faster this way, Bill knew, and safer to be off the road if Charlie Dunn really was on the lookout for him. Also, Bill didn't want to go by his home and risk being seen. There was nothing his mother or sisters could do for Pa right now, and only Doc Hathaway could tell them how serious the wound really was. But the shock of the news would be a dreadful blow. Bill decided that his family would not know what had happened to Pa until he had news, good news, to give them.

He could see Doc Hathaway's cabin now, and

surely that was Doc himself out by the barn? The distant figure paused and turned toward the sound of Prince's thundering hoofbeats. One glance at the horse and rider, and the speed with which they were approaching, and the figure disappeared into the barn. By the time Bill reached it, Doc Hathaway was reemerging with his horse already half saddled. He wasted no time on greetings.

"What is it, Bill, what's happened?" Doc asked, hastily fastening the girth around his horse's belly.

"It's Pa. He got stabbed by a proslaver over at the trading post. Mr. Rively's got him inside, and they're waiting on you."

"Where'd he get hit?" Doc said, mounting his horse.

"Got him in the back," Bill said. Doc nodded.

"We'll just stop at my cabin for my bag," he said, and the two rode swiftly over the path that led to Doc's log house. Bill grabbed the reins and held Doc's horse as he leaped off and dashed into his cabin. Seconds later he came out with a black bag, which he stuffed into a saddlebag. The two horses took off at a gallop, Doc following Bill's lead as he made his way through fields and over streams back toward the trading post.

Though it seemed to take an eternity, they reached the post in less than ten minutes. They quickly tied their horses up, then dashed onto the porch to hammer on the front door.

"Mr. Rively, it's Bill and Doc Hathaway," Bill shouted. By now there were only five or so men still standing around the post. They nodded at Bill and Doc but did not make any move to approach them or to leave. In a moment the front door was unlocked, and Bill and Doc Hathaway hurried inside. Mr. Rively locked the door behind them again.

Pa was still lying on the floor where Bill had left him. Mr. Rively had placed a cushion under his head and had covered him with a blanket. Pa's eyes were closed, and his head angled to one side. Doc knelt by him.

"Isaac? Isaac, can you hear me?" he asked. There was no response. Doc gently rolled Pa to one side to examine the stab wound, ripping his bloody shirt away from the injured area. Bill stood quietly waiting. Doc opened his bag and took several things out. Leaving Pa on his side, he began to clean the wound. Then he took a stethoscope and placed it against Pa's back, listening intently.

"Sounds like it nicked the lung," he said at last. "Wound looks clean enough, but it's gonna be a while before I can say for sure how things are gonna go."

Bill's heart sank. Though he thought he'd prepared himself for anything, he realized he'd been hoping for more encouraging news. Doc Hathaway looked up at Bill.

"What we need is a quiet, safe place for your pa to lay up for a week or two," he said. "Not at home."

"It ain't safe for him here," Mr. Rively said quickly. "This took me by surprise as much as any, but now the first blood has been shed, some of these fellows may not rest until the job is finished. I can control 'em for a spell, but if they know I'm harboring an abolitionist here, they'll turn on me as soon as the next man."

"Well, we wouldn't want that," said Doc Hathaway coldly. "We can take him to my place."

Mr. Rively shook his head. "That's the first place they'll look for him, when they find he's not on his claim. Those who have been suspecting Isaac for an abolitionist have the same suspicions about you, Hathaway."

"Well, I guess they're about to figure out they got two Free-Soilers in Salt Creek Valley," Doc Hathaway said. "Right now, though, all I care about is getting this man away."

"Mr. Rively, can you lend us a wagon?" Bill asked suddenly. The two men turned and looked at him.

"Can you? Can you lend us a wagon?" Bill repeated impatiently. "And some blankets?"

"I reckon I can," Mr. Rively said reluctantly.

"What do you have in mind, Bill?" asked Doc Hathaway.

"I know a place we can take Pa, where he'll be safe. But we'll have to take him on the ferry."

"Where can you mean?" Doc Hathaway asked. Bill glanced at Mr. Rively. He could probably guess where Bill meant, but the boy didn't see any reason to tell him straight out. He might not be the enemy, but he wasn't a friend either.

"Can you get the wagon now?" Bill persisted. "Can you get it set up out back right away?"

Mr. Rively hesitated a moment, then nodded. "All right, then," he said, turning on his heel and heading for the back door.

Pa might not like it, and he might not agree. But it was Bill who had to make the decisions now.

He would take Pa to Uncle Elijah.

Uncle Elijah's face was grim in the flickering candle-light of the upstairs sitting room. He had been deep in conversation with Doc Hathaway for some time and did not appear to be happy with what he was hearing. Periodically he walked to the open door-way leading to the chamber where Pa was resting. He stood in silence for several moments before returning to pace in front of the doctor. They exchanged a few more words; then Uncle Elijah turned and beckoned to Bill, who was seated quietly by the window, his hands balled up into hard fists.

"Yes, sir?" Bill said, walking over to join them.

"The doctor here's done all he can for your pa," Uncle Elijah said, and Doc Hathaway nodded.

"With rest and quiet I give him a good chance at recovering, Bill," Doc Hathaway said.

"But it isn't sensible for Dr. Hathaway to remain here," Uncle Elijah said, sitting down heavily on a wooden chair by the wall. "This is a bad time for his claim to be standing empty.

"And I don't feel at all comfortable knowing your ma and sisters are alone on the claim, without so much as a friendly face for miles around," Uncle Elijah continued. "It's important that Dr. Hathaway get back to Salt Creek Valley as soon as possible. I know a good doctor here in Weston, a man I can trust. Isaac will be in good hands."

Bill could see that Uncle Elijah, as usual, had everything figured out, and this made Bill feel deeply relieved. He inwardly apologized for every time he'd thought his uncle to be high and mighty in the way he took control of things.

There was a slight stirring from the bedroom, and Doc Hathaway headed into the chamber to check on Pa.

Uncle Elijah gave Bill a long look.

"Tell me exactly what happened, son," he said. "Start before the beginning. Did anyone see this coming?"

"No, sir," Bill said, unable to stop the trembling in his voice. He could picture the whole scene clearly, as if it was happening all over again. "We knew the men at Rively's were almost all proslavers, but Pa never spent much time there. He'd be polite to the men when he had to go to the trading post, but he didn't talk to them much, and whenever the talk of slavery would come up, he'd find a way to change the subject. Like you told him to," Bill added. "Pa and I had ridden to Fort Leavenworth so he could talk to the quartermaster about his hay contract, and we had to go straight past Rively's on our way home. There were more men there than I'd seen before, and things seemed rowdier. We tried to ride on by, but some of the men stopped Pa and held his horse and wouldn't keep quiet till they got him up on the speech box to say once and for all if he was proslaver or Free-Soiler."

"And what did he say?" Uncle Elijah asked.

"He didn't get too far," Bill replied. "He had time enough to say he opposed slavery, and then the men started shouting at him, and next thing you know one of them stepped up behind him and plunged a knife straight into his back. I'm not sure Pa ever knew what was happening."

Bill was horrified to feel two fat tears running down his cheek. He rubbed them away quickly.

"Can you tell me anything much about the man who did it?" Uncle Elijah asked gently. "Anything that might help me figure out who he was? Did you get a good look at him?"

"I got better than that. I heard his name a couple of times. Charlie Dunn."

Uncle Elijah looked shocked.

"Charlie Dunn?" he asked. "Are you sure?"

Bill nodded.

"I'm sure, sir. You know the name, then?"

"I know the man. Charlie Dunn works for me. Until today, that is. He'll not work another minute for me. I knew he was pretty fired up about the slavery vote, but I didn't think he was capable of such a thing. Did he know who your pa was?"

"He knew he was kin to you," Bill said. "Mentioned your name, even."

Uncle Elijah stood up and began to pace again, his face a grim mask. Bill wondered if he was angry at having to replace Charlie Dunn. Suddenly he stopped pacing and looked at Bill.

"This is my doing," he said. Bill's eyes widened in surprise.

"What Isaac said to me back before the barbecue was right. I shouldn't have put him on that Vigilance Committee, and I shouldn't have been so certain I knew how things were going to work in Kansas Territory. I overestimated the power of family connections and underestimated the anger of these proslavers. Isaac trusted me, and I didn't give him any choice but to take my advice. And now he's paying for it. You all are."

Bill couldn't think of anything to say, and he thought that he probably wasn't expected to comment. He agreed with what Uncle Elijah was saying, but he hadn't expected his uncle to face up to this so openly. It's himself he's so angry at, Bill thought suddenly. Himself and none other.

"Bill, you did the right thing bringing your father here," Uncle Elijah said, looking at his nephew. "I know that Isaac and I had a falling out, and if Isaac had been conscious, he'd have fought you all the way. I'm proud of you for keeping your head in such a terrible situation."

"Just did what I had to," Bill said, thinking that if his uncle knew how cowardly Bill had actually felt back at Rively's, he might not be very proud. Uncle Elijah shook his head.

"Many would have panicked, Bill, or made a rash decision. You did everything exactly right. You're a smart boy. And judging from what Doc Hathaway has told me, your family is going to need every ounce of your smarts in the days to come."

"Why do you say that, sir?" Bill asked.

"The doctor's feeling is that this is just the beginning," he replied. "That as the election gets closer and closer, there's going to be more ugliness, more violence. From what I can tell, your family and the Hathaways are about the only people not supporting the slavery vote in all of Salt Creek Valley. Plenty of Northerners have come into Kansas, a lot of them from this Emigrant Aid Society, which is sending people from back east to support the Free-Soiler cause. But most of those people have settled south of Fort Leavenworth. Hathaway fears things could get pretty rough for you all. Two weeks ago I'd have laughed it off as impossible, but I see now that things are out of hand. You've got to get back to the claim, Bill, and protect your family."

"And leave Pa?" Bill said, but even as the words came out of his mouth, he knew that he had to.

"I'll see that your pa's taken care of," Uncle Elijah said. "I don't expect you to trust in everything I say anymore, I realize that. But Weston is my home, and I feel safe in assuring you that your pa will be all right here in my house. However, it seems anything could happen in Salt Creek. You're going to have to keep your eyes and ears open, and use that quick brain of yours to keep your family safe. You've got a good head on your shoulders. If anyone can do this, you can."

What Uncle Elijah was saying was frightening. They were going to have to do without Pa for a while. But somehow Ma and the girls had to stay safe. And the crops and horses and animals had to be protected. The Codys had to become a presence on the land; they had to stand strong and be willing to defend themselves against ruffians like Charlie Dunn. At the same time, the farm had to be kept going, the crops tended. And Uncle Elijah was looking to Bill to figure out a way to do it all.

He was only almost nine years old, not much over four and a half feet tall, and his dog Turk probably still outweighed him. What did he have going for him? A quick mind, a keen eye, and a flawless knowledge of the land. And the fastest and smartest horse in Kansas Territory.

What had seemed just weeks ago to be a boring, hard-to-follow political issue had now become a real-life conflict right on Bill's own doorstep. The border ruffians had hurt one of the most important people in the world. And they were threatening everything he and Pa had worked for. Every fence they'd laid, every shingle on the roof, every ear of corn in the field. No matter how hard Pa had tried to avoid it, these men were determined to fight. There was no choice. Bill was just going to have to fight back.

Bill walked over to the doorway and glanced in at the bedchamber. Pa lay still and pale in the bed, Doc Hathaway bending over him gently. In his mind's eye he saw Charlie Dunn thrusting his knife into Pa's back, and Bill felt a deep flash of anger.

He turned to his uncle.

"I'm ready to go."

To his great satisfaction, he realized he was not afraid.

CHAPTER TEN
BORDER RUFFIANS

★   ★   ★

I t was times like this Bill wished he'd never learned to read at all. The newspaper Doc Hathaway had brought over lay open on the kitchen table. Ma sat at the table, a hand covering one side of her face. Julia appeared behind Ma with a freshly brewed cup of coffee, and Martha quietly instructed Eliza Alice to take Mary Hannah and Nellie into Ma's room. When Eliza Alice had disappeared with her charges, Ma folded both her hands in her lap and spoke.

"Read it out loud, Bill," she said in a tired voice.

"Some nasty border ruffian wrote it, Ma,"

Bill protested. "It doesn't—"

"Just read it, Bill," Ma repeated.

He picked up the newspaper and quickly found the part of the article Doc Hathaway had marked.

> "A Mr. Cody, a noisy abolitionist living near Salt Creek in Kansas Territory, was severely stabbed while in a dispute about a claim with Mr. Dunn, on Monday last week. Cody is severely hurt, but not enough it is feared to cause his death. The settlers on Salt Creek regret that his wound is not more dangerous, and all sustain Mr. Dunn in the course he took. Abolitionists will yet find 'Jordan is a hard road to travel'!"

"How can they print such things?" cried Julia. "It's wicked! To say outright they wished that awful man had killed Pa!"

"More than wicked, it's false," Bill added. "There was no dispute about a claim. Those men forced Pa to speak, and Dunn attacked him when he did."

"Well, this confirms what Elijah's letter says," Ma said, taking a sip of the steaming coffee. "Not only can we not expect this man Dunn to be brought to justice, it's more than likely there will be more of the same."

"What are we going to do?" asked Julia.

"Pa mustn't come back here, that's clear," Bill

said. Julia made a sound of protest, but Martha interrupted.

"Bill's right," she said. "We must all pull together to convince him. We may be harassed while we stay here, but it's Pa who's in the most danger. If he returns to the claim, this man Dunn may well try again to kill him."

"I agree," said Ma. "The most important thing of all is Pa's safety. I won't have him risk his life to come home, much as I want him to."

"Couldn't we just leave the claim?" Julia asked.

"And go where?" said Bill. "We can't go back to Iowa; we sold the house and land there months ago. We certainly can't go to Missouri."

"We could go farther south, where those Emigrant Aid Society folks are settling," Julia said. "At least there we'd be with other Free-Soilers, and there's safety in numbers."

"We're not giving up on this land," Bill said, his voice rising. "Pa paid for it, and we've all worked for it, and it's ours."

"I agree," Ma said. "And I know your Pa couldn't stand to just let this claim go. Besides, we could never get a fair price from the proslavers for it, and no Free-Soiler would be crazy enough to move here now. I think our only chance of convincing Pa to stay away from Salt Creek Valley until things calm down is to assure him we'll stay on the land."

"But we have no one to help us," said Julia.

"We have ourselves," Bill said firmly. "And Doc Hathaway's around in a pinch. We can do this, Julia. I can do it," he added. He didn't know much about farming, but their crops had been harvested. And with backbreaking labor and very little sleep, Bill felt pretty sure he could tend to the animals, keep up the buildings, and continue hunting for meat.

"So can I," said Martha without hesitation. Bill thought how many unexpected sides of Martha he'd discovered since they'd left Iowa, and believed her.

Julia still looked anxious, but she nodded.

Ma glanced at the faces of her three oldest children and seemed as pleased as one could under the circumstances. Pa had been recuperating in Weston for almost two weeks. Since that time they'd had several letters from Uncle Elijah updating them on Pa's progress. Though he seemed stronger, he was still having trouble breathing and had not regained much of his strength. No infection or other complications had developed, though, and the Missouri doctor caring for Pa felt optimistic about his eventual recovery.

But as Pa recovered in Elijah's house, the mood outside was becoming more and more explosive. Through reading newspaper accounts or from what Doc Hathaway picked up from other people, Bill was well aware of the rising tensions in Kansas Territory. The Emigrant Aid folks Julia had suggested they go live near had already had a few rough run-ins with proslavers in Lawrence. Doc Hathaway had told Bill about an argument between a proslavery man and Free-Soiler that ended with one man killing the other. And newspapers and gossips alike reported that Missourians were pouring into Kansas Territory every day. Bill had wondered about their Senator Atchison, who was plainly telling folks from Missouri to cross over and do anything they had to, to get the slave-state vote passed.

"We can do anything if we stick together as a family," Ma said. "I will write to your Pa today and tell him we want to keep the claim, and convince him to stay well away from Salt Creek, at least until this election is over and done with."

"When will that be?" Julia asked.

"It's scheduled for end of November, they say," Bill replied. "Maybe six weeks from now."

"And you think things will be quiet again after the election is over?" Julia asked a little anxiously.

This kind of question usually would have been put to Pa. Bill noticed with a little pride that, in Pa's absence, Julia had automatically asked Bill instead. He made a serious and thoughtful face.

"We can only hope so," Ma said to Julia, before Bill could say anything.

"But we mustn't count on it," Bill threw in quickly,

and they all looked at him.

"We have to be prepared for the worst, and we have to be ready. They may come after us, and they may come soon."

They did come, sooner than anyone thought.

Several days later Bill and Julia made a quick visit to Opkee's village, some six miles west of the Codys' cabin. It was an official visit, for Bill was there to make some trades with the Kickapoo. It was no longer safe for any Cody to go to Rively's. Opkee also told them what prairie plants were safe to eat and where they were most likely to find berries and nuts growing. Though Bill ached to linger with Opkee, and to put his troubles behind him for just an hour, he knew they must get home as quickly as possible. And by the way Julia was now treating him, with a mix of respect and obedience, he knew she expected him to keep their excursion strictly to business. They were a long way from the days when Julia would allow Bill to talk her into wandering off the path for a quick game of Lewis and Clark.

It was as they approached their land, side by side in their saddles, that Julia and Bill first saw the clouds of dark smoke curling into the sky. Prince whickered softly.

"What is it?" Julia cried. "Oh, Bill, is it the house?"

"It's not the house," said Bill, gesturing for Julia to stop her horse. "It's the hay."

Bill pointed, and Julia could see them now. Three men on horseback were dashing back and forth between the piles of dried hay Bill and Pa had made. At each stack they would pause, lighting the dried grass with burning torches. In moments the accumulated work of months went up in smoke. The sale of the hay to the fort was to have provided the Codys with a great deal of money, money they needed even more desperately now that Pa required daily medical attention. And in the blink of an eye it was taken from them. The days and days of exhausting work, now for nothing.

Bill and Julia watched the smoke rising silently, making the mounted figures become less visible through the dark haze. Then, as Bill hoped, the men suddenly turned their horses and rode quickly away from their cabin.

"They're not going for the cabin," Bill said. "Let's go!"

He brought Prince to a gallop as they headed for their home. Though Bill was relieved to see the men departing, he did not confide his fear to Julia that they might have gone into the cabin *before* setting the hay alight. Urging Prince to go even faster, he refused to allow the thought of what might have happened to his family to enter his mind. He would allow himself to think only about what he could do now.

As the children galloped toward the house, Bill

saw with relief it was untouched. The front door was open, and Ma and Martha rushed out with buckets. Bill waved at them, bringing Prince directly to the front door and jumping off the horse before he'd come to a full stop. Julia was several moments behind him.

"Did they come in? Are you all right?" Bill panted, out of breath.

Ma put her arms around Bill and hugged him tightly. From inside the house where he'd been leashed, Turk was barking loudly. Loose outside, Turk would be a tempting target for those up to no good.

"We didn't even know they were outside, Bill, until Turk started up. Then we smelled the smoke," Ma said. "Thank God you're all right. I was so afraid you'd return before they rode off. We must get water!"

Bill shook his head and put his hand out to stop Martha, who was moving forward.

"It's too late," he said. "The hay is gone. No sense in setting ourselves on fire as well. I'll make sure it isn't spreading, but that's moist soil around those haystacks. Best to let them just burn themselves out."

Ma nodded. Even Ma trusts me to take control of things, Bill thought in amazement. How had this happened? Why were they all so willing to put their faith in him? He tried not to think about it. He had fires to tend to.

Bill walked out to examine the smoldering haystacks by himself. The sight of the ruined stacks seemed an ominous symbol. What had appeared solid and real and full of promise was now nothing but ash.

Had it been just four months ago that he had set out alongside Pa to turn the sod and plant their first crops? Had it been just two weeks ago that they'd ridden to Fort Leavenworth to see the quartermaster, full of optimism and hope for their future? Now things looked bleaker than they ever had before, even when Sammy had died. Though he did everything he could to remain strong to his ma and sisters, Bill secretly wondered whether they *could* survive this without Pa. The way they seemed to have placed their confidence in him so completely was frightening to Bill. Did they honestly think he could do it?

The sound of hoofbeats brought Bill to attention. He anxiously scanned the landscape and spotted two mounted riders heading in the direction of the cabin. He could have kicked himself for being taken unawares. When the border ruffians had sped off after lighting the fires, Bill had assumed the family was now safe. Inside the cabin Ma and his sisters would no longer be on the lookout for trouble. Even at a dead run it would take Bill a minute or two to reach the house. And if the horsemen caught sight of him and took their horses to a canter, they could cut him off before he could even get inside. What should he do? Bill ran the options over in his mind wildly, but he saw no solution but to walk steadily toward the house, showing no outward signs of fear.

As he began walking, he noticed one of the riders seemed to be sitting rather sloppily in the saddle. It looked from a distance as though the fellow might be drunk, a bad sign indeed. A tumble of thoughts sped through his mind. He should never leave the house unarmed, nor should he ever leave Ma without a weapon. He should have emergency supplies hidden on the land—food, lanterns, blankets, additional weapons, in the event someone was caught outside. He should make sure Turk was always inside the cabin when he left, to give warning of strangers without making himself a target of gunfire. But why were all these thoughts coming to him *now*, with two ruffians closing in on his unprotected family?

As the riders drew closer, Bill got a better look. The horses were unfamiliar, and he couldn't make out much of the drooping rider, but the other was coming into better view. Bill stopped suddenly in his tracks. Then he took off at a run, shouting in the direction of the cabin.

"It's Pa!" he called. "It's Uncle Elijah and Pa!"

The door to the cabin flew open, and Ma and Julia almost collided with Bill as the horses came to a stop before them. Ma and Bill were at Pa's side instantly, and Uncle Elijah leaped off his own horse and helped

Pa carefully out of the saddle.

"What happened?" Pa said in a strange, wheezing voice, looking across the fields to the still-smoking stacks of hay.

"Three men on horseback rode through with torches and set them alight," Bill replied. "They left just fifteen minutes ago. It's a miracle you didn't cross their path."

"Did you get a look at them, Bill?" asked Uncle Elijah.

"Not enough to know who they were," Bill said.

"Did they harm any of you? Threaten you?" Uncle Elijah asked. Pa looked eager to hear the answer to this question, but it seemed too great an effort for him to speak.

"No, sir," Bill said. "Julia and I were a mile or so off, riding back from the Kickapoo village where we were getting some supplies. We held off getting any closer when we saw them, and waited till they rode off before heading to the cabin."

"Turk gave us a good warning," Ma said. "We stayed out of sight."

Ma had her arm around Pa's waist and began gently leading him toward the house. Though Bill knew Ma was happy to see Pa, he could tell she was worried that he'd come back to Salt Creek Valley. It worried Bill, too. But no one mentioned it. Instead the family made a little circle around Pa as he moved slowly along, encouraging him with smiles and soft words.

Bill caught sight of Eliza Alice framed in the doorway, her narrow face looking anxious and confused at the sight of Pa. She was holding Nellie tightly by the hand. Bill hurried over to them and made a gesture to Julia, who came as well.

"It's all right, Eliza Alice," Bill said. "Step in for a moment; they'll be at the doorway soon."

"You remember we told you Pa was hurt in an accident," Julia said to Eliza Alice, who nodded.

"I remember," Nellie piped in. She looked worried too, but in a more excited way than Eliza Alice.

"Well, Pa got well enough to come home," Bill said. "But we'll have to take good care of him, and make extra certain we get our chores done and keep the house neat and quiet."

"He's not going to die?" Nellie asked, more matter-of-fact than in fear. She had recently expressed a good deal of interest in the subject of death, even bringing home a dead bird and giving a short speech on the possible manner of its demise.

"I don't think so, Nellie-Belle," Bill said. Ma and Pa were coming through the doorway now, Uncle Elijah close behind them.

"Can you take Nellie upstairs to the loft?" Julia asked Eliza Alice softly.

Nellie looked angry at the suggestion, but Eliza

Alice nodded with relief. Bill knew that Eliza Alice hated anything unpleasant or out of the ordinary.

Martha poked her head in the doorway just long enough to announce she'd stabled the horses and was going to fetch Doc Hathaway. Bill kicked himself that he hadn't had the good sense to fetch the doctor himself.

"I'll just get him comfortable in our room," Ma said to Uncle Elijah. "Julia, can you see to your uncle for a moment?"

"Yes, Ma," Julia said. She took Uncle Elijah's coat and hat and hung them on some pegs by the door.

"You must be hungry after your ride. Or thirsty?" Julia said, but Uncle Elijah just shook his head.

"How are *you*, Bill?" Uncle Elijah asked.

Bill felt pleased to be asked but embarrassed for Julia. After all, she'd been on the ride, too, and was standing right in front of them now. Why wasn't Uncle Elijah including her in the question? Bill tried to shoot Julia a sympathetic look before answering, but she avoided his glance.

"I was more annoyed with myself than anything else, sir," Bill said honestly. "If those men had a mind to burn our hay, there wasn't anything I could have done about it. But I didn't realize till I saw them we need to be more prepared."

Uncle Elijah nodded as Ma came in, pulling the bedroom door softly shut behind her.

"He's sleeping, right alongside Mary Hannah. She

never even stirred from her nap, bless her."

"Martha has gone for the doctor," Uncle Elijah said.

"Good. But for heaven's sake, Elijah, why did you bring him here? From your letters I thought you understood my position."

"I understood it perfectly, Mary, and agreed with it. I still do. I told Isaac so, and in the beginning he listened. But with the election getting closer, he grew more and more determined to come home. And frankly, Mary, I felt I owed him. He's in trouble in large part due to my bad counsel. In good conscience I can hardly refuse to let him do now what he thinks best."

Ma sighed.

"I'm happy to see him, of course, and grateful for your help," she said. "But oh, Elijah, after what happened today, I do wish he was safely back in Weston!"

"You said Pa grew more insistent about returning home as the election got closer?" Bill asked. At the beginning of the summer Bill never would have dreamed of inserting himself into a conversation between adults, particularly when one of them was his uncle Elijah. But things were different now.

"That's right, Bill," replied Uncle Elijah.

"But surely he doesn't . . . that is, Pa can't be meaning to go and vote, can he?" Bill asked. Uncle Elijah sat suddenly back in his chair.

"Goodness, I hadn't even thought of that," he replied. "And Isaac certainly didn't come out and say so, but you may well be right, Bill. Isaac's begun to follow these politics very closely. He said since he almost lost his life for being a Free-Soiler, he now means to start acting like one."

"But we can't let him!" Ma said. "He'll be one of the only no votes in the whole district—he'll be torn to pieces!"

Ma and Uncle Elijah both turned to look at Bill expectantly. Even Uncle Elijah seemed to acknowledge Bill's new position in their family, he thought. Bill didn't think he'd ever get used to that idea. But they were waiting for him to answer.

"After coming all this way, he's not likely to take no for an answer," Bill said slowly, looking from Ma to Uncle Elijah. "And he is my pa. If he asks me straight out to help him go, I don't know that I can refuse him."

And that seemed to be good enough for them.

CHAPTER ELEVEN
WAITING

★　　★　　★

The first frost had come, and the ground had begun to harden in the chilly autumn air. Tingling winds blew constantly from the west, seeming to cleanse the entire landscape. Everything seemed brighter, crisper, and tantalizingly new. Bill was working harder than he'd ever worked in his life—rising before dawn each day and toiling steadily through dusk to get the work of father and son done by himself. But he had

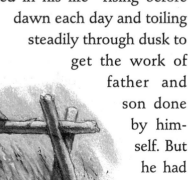

never felt better, or stronger. Ma said he was growing about an inch a day. His legs and arms seemed longer and more powerful than they had just months ago. Though the world around him threatened to explode at any moment, the days seemed curiously peaceful, and their claim magically protected from all danger.

On a day such as this it was almost possible for Bill to believe that there was no unpleasantness in the world. Two weeks had passed since the burning of the hay, and so far the border ruffians had not returned. Pa was feeling better, and the wound in his back was healing without infection, though he had still not recovered any ease of breathing and the slightest exertion tired him out. Doc Hathaway called on them faithfully each day, bringing not only his doctor's skills but the latest newspapers and rumors.

Outside the Cody family, only two people in Kansas Territory knew Pa was secretly recuperating at home—Doc Hathaway and Opkee. In the weeks that had followed Pa's return, Opkee had paid many visits, often bringing food and supplies the Codys could not buy or trade for themselves now that they avoided Rively's trading post. It was Opkee Bill was waiting for this morning, as the bright November sun illuminated the landscape with its peculiar fresh fall light.

Bill now never strayed farther from the cabin than

absolutely necessary, so he perched on a fence rail by the barn and scanned the landscape for the sight of Opkee. Almost by magic he appeared, his pony trotting energetically up the hill past the spring.

Bill jumped off the fence and waved happily. Opkee waved back, easily balanced on the pony's bare back as he bounced contentedly along. When he got to the fence, he swung lightly down from his pony's back and handed Bill a cloth bag he had been carrying.

"Neota's cakes," he said, and Bill's mouth began to water.

"Ma will be delighted," Bill said. "Everyone's inside—they'll be happy to see you. But let's sit out here a spell. I've been at my chores since before sunrise, and I could use a break."

They leaned against the fence, splitting one of Neota's cakes and munching for several moments in silence.

"Your pa is growing stronger?" Opkee asked, when he had swallowed his last mouthful of cake.

"I think so," Bill said. "The paste you gave us to put on his back seems to have helped. But he still can't get his breath or move about easily. And the proslavers still want to hurt him, and in his state it would be an easy job."

"And this election, it will bring out these bad men?" asked Opkee.

Bill nodded. "Doc Hathaway's heard some saying they mean to shoot any man not voting for slavery. In the newspaper Senator Atchison himself says if he had his way, he'd hang every abolitionist who dared show his face in Kansas Territory. A senator is a kind of chief," he added.

"Good chief, bad chief," Opkee said. "Kickapoo also have the same. That is why the Kickapoo chief called Kishko took his people to Mexico. He and Kennekuk each thought the other a bad chief."

"I wish Senator Atchison would take his folks to Mexico," Bill said ruefully. "But he's bringing them all here, is what he's doing. There's other folks like us down in Lawrence, but up here people mostly come over from Missouri to vote proslave."

"Senator Atchison's men sound like a bad tribe," Opkee said. "Like Kiowa or Comanche."

But Bill shook his head vehemently.

"They really aren't," he said. "My uncle Elijah has lived in Missouri for years, and he's a decent fellow. His friends and acquaintances too. I reckon there's just as many good folks in Missouri as there ever were back in Iowa. Problem is, the bad ones have gotten all riled up, and come over here with their guns and knives and whiskey. Kind of easy to lose sight of all the decent folks they left at home, while they're making such a ruckus here."

"I understand this," Opkee said. "It is the same in

our tribe. My people keep to Kennekuk's way, but many other Kickapoo do not. They raise the tomahawk, or drink whiskey, or make themselves enemy to the white man. They fight with their own tribe, and live in a way Kennekuk did not like at all. But still, they are Kickapoo. We are Kickapoo. The same, but different."

"Yes," said Bill. "That's it exactly. Unfortunately, we're real outnumbered here. Sometimes I just don't know what I'll do when the border ruffians come back. And I know they're coming back."

"Weak men have dull eyes and bad minds," Opkee said. "You lead them where you want them to go, make them see what you want them to see. One Bill is closer to the Great Spirit than all these ruffians. You have the power to make the spells."

"Do you really think so?" Bill asked earnestly. "There's just one of me."

"Just one of Kennekuk, too. It took only one."

And Opkee gave one of his slightly superior looks. But his words stayed with Bill. It took only one.

Chapter Twelve
TESTED

★   ★   ★

It occurred to Bill, not for the first time that month, that life was a funny thing. How many hours had he spent back in Iowa with Joe Barnes and Sammy, playing scout and watching the landscape for hours for any one of the imaginary dangers their minds had placed nearby. Bill could clearly remember the excitement of those games, and could remember as well the longing to experience, just once, some real danger.

Ma was fond of warning Bill to be careful what he wished for. At last Bill was in the position to understand exactly what she meant.

Because he'd gotten what he'd thought he wanted. He was a real scout now, constantly on the lookout for invaders. The stakes were as real and high as they came. Everything depended on Bill's remaining alert, on the keenness of his eye and the sharpness of his instincts. And having got what he wished for, Bill found it was not, in fact, exhilarating. It was not exciting to do the chores of two grown men, all the while keeping eyes and ears open for the sound of any possible invasion. It was not satisfying to feel that the well-being of the people he loved best in the world was at risk. His back ached, his head throbbed, and his mind felt numb with the exhaustion of never, even for an instant, letting down his guard. Yet Bill felt a sense of pride that he had never known before. And he kept working, and he kept watching.

His vigilance paid off, because when the border ruffians finally returned, Bill saw them from a good distance. He was ready. Dropping his shovel where he had been working by the stables, he ran for the house and burst through the front door.

"They're coming!" he shouted. "Everyone, quick! They're coming!"

He had plotted each move, assigned each member

of the family his or her part down to the very smallest detail. They had practiced again and again, until Bill was satisfied that the whole thing could be accomplished in less time than it took a rider to crest the hill of their claim.

Julia grabbed a long skirt and bonnet hanging by the door and rushed into the room where Pa lay. Martha cleared the cabin of any evidence of Pa's presence, tossing his pipe into a box and folding a pair of pants she'd been mending and thrusting them into a drawer. Eliza Alice was nervously reminding Nellie of the absolute importance of saying that Pa was not home, had not been home for some time, and that she believed him to be recovering from a riding accident in Weston. Bill had his shotgun squirreled away upstairs. Just as he turned to call for Julia to hurry, she came out of the bedroom with Pa.

She had helped him pull the long skirt over his britches and was tying the bonnet under his newly shaven chin. It should have been a silly sight, but for the knowledge that the success of the disguise might save Pa's very life. As to Pa himself, he looked pale and grave, leaning heavily on Julia for support.

"Wait here," Bill said, opening the door to the cabin and peering out. The riders were coming fast, but Bill guessed they were still a good three or four minutes away. He turned to his father and sister quickly.

"There's time, but you must hurry," Bill said.

Julia led Pa to the door and handed him the empty bucket waiting there for this moment. She also picked up an ax, her designated weapon. With shaking hands Pa tucked his own revolver under his shawl. Bill pulled the door open. Julia looked frightened, but her jaw was set in determination and her grip on the ax handle firm.

"Don't worry," she said quickly. "We've practiced enough times. I know where to go."

"Be careful, Bill," Pa said in his labored and breathless way.

"We'll be fine. Now go, go!"

Pa and Julia walked slowly but steadily outside and toward the cornfield. The approaching ruffians would simply see two women on their way to fetch some water. Nothing that would particularly grab their attention or divert them from their goal of reaching the cabin. Though Bill thought the two figures looked terribly small and unprotected, he knew the disguise should be protection enough. He had made it a point to be aware of every instance of violence and aggression that had taken place in the territory, and he knew that so far the border ruffians had stopped short of causing any physical harm to women or children. If they could be made to believe that Pa was really not home, if they persisted in believing that only two insignificant women had left the house, the Codys should ultimately be left alone. Bill had not forgotten Opkee's words about bad men and weak minds. Bill did not believe that all bad men were so deceivable, but he did believe in his own ability to pull the wool over the eyes of these angry border ruffians.

With a last quick look in the cabin, Bill was convinced that everything was set according to his plan. Eliza Alice had taken Nellie and Mary Hannah into Ma and Pa's room, where she spread out her mending work on the bed. She sat studiously by the window, her head bent over her sewing, as Nellie and Mary Hannah played with their corncob dolls. Turk was curled at the foot of the bed, his ears pricked and his body tense, but mindful of Bill's repeated instructions to stay quiet. In the kitchen Ma and Martha set to baking. Bill went outside to the stables and retrieved his shovel. Holding it in one hand, he turned toward the approaching riders as if becoming aware of them for the first time. He took a deep breath and stood ready.

He recognized Charlie Dunn straightaway, and Earl who rode beside him. The other two men were strangers. Their unshaven faces and worn clothes could have belonged to any of a hundred men Bill had seen around Rively's.

Charlie Dunn rode over to Bill, dismounting right in front of the boy.

"I come for the old man, and I mean to have him," Charlie Dunn said, squinting at Bill. "He inside?"

"He's not here," Bill said, noticing the long knife tucked into Charlie Dunn's britches. The same knife, no doubt, that had wounded Pa so terribly.

"Don't believe ya," Charlie Dunn said, motioning to Earl and the two others to dismount.

"I tell you, he ain't here," Bill said. "He's needed quite a bit of doctoring, and he's laying up across the river."

"Yeah, I heard tell your pa suffered an unfortunate accident," Charlie Dunn said with an unpleasant smile. "My aim ain't as good as I thought, but I'm ready to finish the job sure enough."

"He ain't here," Bill repeated, swallowing the feeling of hatred for Charlie Dunn that was rising in his throat.

"I'm sure you won't mind if I take a look myself," Charlie Dunn said, still smiling his ugly smile. "Joe, you tie up the horses and go check the barn and outhouse. Earl, you scout around outside. You come along inside with me, Mike."

Much as he wanted to, Bill wouldn't let himself so much as glance in the direction in which Pa and Julia had set off. He knew exactly where they should be, in the little bushy grove a quarter of a mile past the edge of the cornfield. Bill had laid in a cache of blankets, food, water, and lanterns there, in case they had to wait it out for some time.

As Charlie Dunn and his fellow ruffian headed for the cabin, Bill followed them. Dunn gave a sharp laugh.

"Come along then, little soldier," he said. "March right alongside me—I don't care. But if I find your pa inside, boy, I mean to have him and there ain't nothing you can do to stop me."

"There's nobody inside but my ma and sisters," Bill said calmly.

"Everybody inside, then?"

Bill felt he was being tested and shook his head. "Two of my sisters are out fetching berries and water. The rest are inside doing chores, with Ma."

"All alone, with no man to protect 'em?" Charlie Dunn asked mockingly. They were at the front door now.

"They got me to protect them," Bill said, and Charlie Dunn and Mike shouted with laughter as they pushed open the door.

Inside, Ma looked up from her baking and stood up.

"What can I do for you men?" she asked quietly.

"You know good and well what I come for," Charlie Dunn said. "I aim to take that cussed abolitionist husband of yours."

Ma gestured around the cabin with both hands.

"See for yourself, Mr. . . . Dunn, isn't it? It's just Bill and the girls here these many weeks."

"Don't mind if I do," Charlie Dunn said, glancing at Martha, who had continued kneading dough as if nothing was going on. "Don't mind at all if I do."

The cabin was small, and it didn't take much time for Charlie Dunn to search through it. Bill followed him into Ma and Pa's bedroom, standing behind him as he made a great show of looking under the bed. Eliza Alice sewed furiously, her face pale and her lips pinched. Bill tried to throw her a reassuring look, but she wouldn't look up. Mary Hannah was napping in blissful ignorance, but Nellie watched Charlie Dunn intently, her eyes wide. Charlie Dunn's gaze fell on her.

"Well, now, little girl, what's that you got there?"

"My dollie," Nellie said, clutching the corncob doll to her chest protectively.

"She got a name?" Charlie Dunn asked.

"Frances," Nellie replied. "And I'm Nellie."

Why did she have to be so darn friendly? Bill wondered anxiously. But at the same time, if Nellie could get through this little conversation, it might make the whole thing look more convincing.

"Well, Nellie, where's your pa today?" Charlie Dunn asked.

Bill felt as if his heart had jumped right into his throat. Nellie gave a little sigh, pushed out her lower lip slightly, and said, "Pa ain't been home for the longest spell. I don't know how much sadder I can be."

"Did he go away?" Charlie Dunn asked, glancing at Eliza Alice, whose needle had frozen mid stitch. Nellie gave a serious nod.

"He had a accident," she said importantly. "He went and found a really good doctor, but the doctor's making him stay in bed!"

"Won't let him come home, huh?" Charlie Dunn pressed. Bill was almost beside himself with anxiety, shifting his weight from one foot to the other. But Nellie looked quite unruffled. She seemed to be almost enjoying herself. She gave another little sigh and arranged her face in a woebegone expression.

"No, he won't and won't. And when he does, I expect he'll be too tired to bring me a present." She looked at Charlie Dunn through her long eyelashes. "I guess it's wicked of me to want a present. Do you think so, mister?"

Charlie Dunn looked slightly embarrassed.

"I don't reckon so, little miss. I don't reckon so much."

With that he turned and walked out of the room.

"He ain't in there, Mike. What's upstairs?" he called.

Bill paused long enough to take in Nellie's eager face. Only a four-year-old could want a review of her performance at this harrowing moment, but the fact was, Nellie had been superb. Bill blew her a kiss, and she caught it and pressed it to her smiling mouth with little fists. Then he ran out to follow Charlie Dunn up the narrow staircase to the second floor.

There was just the one room upstairs. Charlie Dunn made a show of walking to and fro, his head coming close to the rafter on which Bill had stowed his shotgun. This weapon would remain hidden, and Bill would use it only as a last recourse, if any of the men turned violent. Otherwise it would remain stowed away, for if Charlie Dunn knew of its presence, he would simply take it.

After what seemed like an eternity, Charlie Dunn finally seemed satisfied that Isaac Cody was not to be found. He paused by the front door, glancing at Ma but addressing his words to Bill.

"I ain't found him here, and maybe you're telling the truth and maybe you ain't. Don't really matter. You just tell that blackheart that I'm looking for him, and I aim to keep looking until I find him. You just make sure he knows that, wherever he is."

Bill didn't move a muscle, and the two men walked outside. Bill stood at the door, watching them as they walked over to join their friends by the stable. What he saw next almost wrenched out his heart.

The man called Jack was leading Prince out of the stable. The other three examined the horse and nodded and gestured, and when they climbed back onto their own horses, they began to lead Prince off with them. The horse was whinnying and bucking, but the men pulled him harshly along. Every muscle in Bill's body screamed for action, for movement, for a mad dash outside to save his precious horse. But Bill fought to keep still. The men were leaving. They had not damaged anything or anyone in the house. They were riding off in the opposite direction from Julia and Pa's hiding place in the cornfield. The last thing Bill should do was make any scene that might cause them to return.

"Prince!" Bill whispered, watching the men lead him away.

CHAPTER THIRTEEN

THE VOTE

★   ★   ★

Bill didn't like to think what might have happened if the letter hadn't come when it did. Pa wanted so much to vote in that election. The border ruffians continued their visits every few days or so, and still Pa refused to leave. But then the letter came, just days shy of the election, and everything changed.

Bill had never met the Mr. Whitney who had written the letter, but he had heard the name before. Mr. Whitney was one of the few Free-Soilers with a real presence in northeastern Kansas Territory. Pa had spoken well of him, mentioning his sharp business instincts and healthy savings. Mr. Whitney wrote that he and three other gentlemen had decided to locate and develop a new town site in Kansas Territory. Pa's reputation in surveying the land was widely known, and the men wished him to join them as an equal partner in exchange for his expertise.

The area in which the men were interested lay thirty or forty miles west of the Codys' claim. Unlike Salt Creek Valley, this area was much more sparsely populated, and prime land was still available. Equally appealing was the fact that the border ruffians seemed to be concentrating their activities on the easternmost portion of the territory, and settlers farther west were witnessing considerably less of the conflict between Free-Soilers and proslavers.

Though Pa wanted to actively participate in Free-Soil politics, he was at heart a seeker of new opportunities. It was one of the things he told Bill he thought greatest about their country—that there were so many different chances in life for a man to make something of himself, if only he knew to jump at those chances when they arose.

Bill knew Pa had done his share of jumping at chances. He remembered Pa as a farmer, a stagecoach driver, a politician, and a land developer. Pa had even joined a small party going out west to join the California gold rush, but illness had turned his party back. Pa had seized each of these opportunities, and if none of them had made him a rich man, each had in its own way made him a happier one. The possibility of joining a partnership to start up a new town site was something Bill knew Pa wouldn't want to pass up. So though it meant missing the opportunity to vote, and though his strength was still only about half what it should be, Pa immediately accepted the offer.

There was much to be done, but somehow Pa found the time to take a walk with Bill along the edge of the cornfields the morning he was to depart. For a while they simply strolled in silence, Pa occasionally leaning on Bill for support.

"This ain't how I imagined things would be, Bill," Pa said at last, looking off over their land into the distance.

Bill looked at his father expectantly.

"When I staked this claim and bought this land, I meant it to be our home for a long time to come. I never imagined a day would come when our family would be split. I should have seen it coming, should have taken heed of the warning signs, but I didn't."

Bill thought that after all that had gone on, Pa expected him to speak frankly.

"I don't see how you could have known how

ugly it would all get, Pa. I don't see how any of us could have known. You just did what Uncle Elijah thought was best."

But Pa shook his head.

"I can't accept that, son. I've put a lot of blame on my brother in my life, none more than these past few months. But that was just the easy way out. I'm a grown man, and I ought to be responsible for whatever choices I make. When I think of it now, I realize how many folks warned us when we were crossing Iowa and Missouri, how many said this whole situation might be a whole lot hotter than I thought. Fact is, Bill, I came to Kansas Territory to farm land, and I didn't pay much attention to anyone or anything that might be trying to tell me things were going to be hard. And that's my fault, not Elijah's or anyone else's."

"Well, Uncle Elijah admits now that he didn't see how things truly were going to be in Kansas Territory," Bill argued.

"And neither did I," Pa said. "It's easy to blame your problems on somebody else, but I'm not gonna do it anymore. I make the decisions, nobody else. I can learn from my mistakes. I just wish you didn't have to, Bill."

"I don't understand," said Bill.

They had reached the northwest corner of the cornfield. Beyond it was the grove where Pa and

Julia had hidden during the border ruffians' raids. They paused there and turned back to face the corn-field and the cabin and barn beyond it. So much of what they had accomplished was there for the looking—the buildings sturdy and bright in the November sun, the plowed land waiting for new crops.

"You and your ma and sisters have all lost a lot this past year. Your brother, your old home, your horse you love so, and now your pa. But for you, Bill, it's something even more. I've watched you change and grow since we left Iowa, and I've seen you taking up responsibilities here in Kansas Territory that many grown men would shy from. And I want you to know how proud that makes me, Bill. I wouldn't have thought I could leave Ma and the girls here on their own. But I've come to realize these past months that you have everything a good man should—strength, brains, good instinct, and most of all loyalty. You're the kind of son every man dreams of having." Pa paused for a moment, catch-ing his breath. "But at the same time, I can't help feeling you've lost something in all this. Back in Iowa, you'd have spent much of your time playing with Joe and Sammy, down by the river with the steamboat pilots. You did your share of the work, sure, but you had your share of fun too. And there just don't seem to be much fun for you in life right now, and I'm so sorry for that."

Bill glowed with his father's words of praise while at the same time feeling embarrassed. He ducked his head and thought about what Pa said. He did miss Joe. He missed their games and mischief. He missed the opportunity to indulge his sense of adventure and imagination. He missed being carefree.

"But I don't think I'd change it, Pa," Bill finally said. "Everything you say is right, and a lot of it I've thought of myself. And if you'd asked me back in Iowa if I could give it all up, I reckon I'd have said no. But we're not in Iowa anymore, and this is my life now, for better or worse. For better, I think. Maybe I am growing up before my time. And it sure ain't easy. But it feels right, somehow. Like something I'm meant to do, something I was born for."

Pa nodded. "There's always a few folks, Bill, who're meant for more than others. In my heart I always felt you were one of them. And here you are, already proving me right."

Bill felt his face grow hot. Privately he wondered if he would truly measure up to such lofty hopes. But Pa's praise felt so sweet, Bill wanted to gather up the words and hoard them as if they were treasure.

They didn't speak of these things again. They didn't need to. They slowly walked back to the cabin. Mr. Whitney and one of his partners, Mr. Jolly, came for Pa at the appointed time. Ma and the girls were sad but resolute. Ma, Julia, and Martha all believed firmly that Pa was going to a much safer place and so were willing to relinquish him. Eliza Alice wore her customary expression of anxiety, but long ago the family had accepted that she liked to be kept as much in the dark as possible. Details, the reasons behind things, and the expectations for what might take place worried her endlessly. Pa had stayed with them for a spell, and now he was to stay in another place. Beyond this, Eliza Alice sought no information. Nellie was imitating the brave faces of her oldest sisters, but her lower lip trembled in a telltale way.

"Oh, Nellie-Belle," Pa said, kneeling beside his daughter. "Next time I come home, I reckon I'll be strong enough to pick you up and twirl you around like I used to."

Nellie looked stricken.

"Buh—Bill says I'm growing like a weed!" she said, giving in to tears. "Won't I be too big?"

Pa shook his head and hugged Nellie tight.

"You'll never be too big for me to twirl, Nellie. Now you mind your ma and Bill. He's gonna be the man of the house while I'm gone."

Nellie nodded seriously.

"All right then," Pa said, rising slowly to his feet.

They had really said their good-byes around the breakfast table, and Bill thought the last thing Pa's new partners should see was a weeping family cling-ing to their newly appointed surveyor. So he set the example by quickly shaking Pa's hand, then stepping back. Pa looked his family over and gave them a final smile and nod, then climbed into Little Gray's saddle. Two weeks ago he hadn't been strong enough to saddle the horse up himself. So though Pa's move-ments looked oddly slow and pained, Bill knew that Pa was actually stronger than he'd been since Charlie Dunn had stabbed him. He was going to be all right.

The colder it got, the hotter the news. Rumors spread fast and fierce, all faithfully reported to Bill by Doc Hathaway. Bill could barely keep up with it all. It was beyond him how it had come down to this, with folks so convinced of their own rightness that they threatened to hurt or kill anyone not on their side. Had everyone lost their minds over this vote? Doc showed Bill a long newspaper article warning: "If we cannot do this, it is an omen that the institution of slavery must fall in this and the other Southern states, but it would fall after much strife, civil war, and bloodshed." It was the first time Bill had heard the dire prediction that his country could turn and declare war with itself over the issue of slavery. Was there enough madness, Bill wondered, to ignite an entire nation to violence?

In the days before the election, voters poured in

by the hundreds, and as far as Doc Hathaway could tell, just about every new arrival north of Fort Leavenworth was loudly and brazenly proslavery. On horse, by the wagon load, or on foot, they came, swearing each to cast his own vote and to shoot down any man voting Free-Soil. Bill had asked Doc if there weren't some rules about who could vote and who couldn't. Surely a man couldn't simply show up and vote when he clearly was not a resident of the territory.

There were rules, Doc had explained, and they stated quite plainly that a voter had to be an actual resident of Kansas Territory. But, Doc told Bill, the rules were being ignored. The entire process had gone to pieces before it had even begun, and there didn't seem to be a thing to be done about it.

Bill stayed home on the day of the election. He wasn't old enough to vote, of course. You had to be twenty-one. He did hope that on election day of all days the Cody claim would be left in peace, and it was. All day of November 29 Bill kept watch anxiously, and he never saw a soul approach.

He learned the results of the election the very next day. The proslavers had won by a landslide, 2,258 to 305. Kansas Territory had taken its first step toward becoming a slave state. Doc Hathaway had been prevented from voting at all—the mob of proslavery men simply closed in a tight circle around the voting place and would not let him enter. Such things had happened all over the territory. Men who had no right to vote had cast ballots ten or twenty times over. Others who really lived in the Territory were kept away with threats or bullied into changing their votes.

It all made Bill's head spin. And worst of everything, this election had not decided the entire matter once and for all. Bill had been wrong about that. Another election, for the Territorial Legislature, was scheduled for March of the following year. And already, Doc told Bill, the two sides were gearing up to fight, to do whatever they could, whatever they had to, in order to win.

Bill trudged out over the first light snowfall of the season. Opkee's people had warned that a bitter winter would soon be upon them. That would quiet folks, Bill knew. They'd have enough to do just keeping their hearth fires burning and their stomachs full. But then what? Would things really get ugly again when this new election in March came around? Bill just couldn't bring himself to believe it. No, Bill thought as he checked the stable to make sure the snow was staying out, surely things would cool down now that the snow had come. Tempers had flared, hearts had grown hot, but such extremes never lasted long. Look at Pa and Uncle Elijah, Bill thought. They're okay now. They weren't, and now they are. Simple as that.

Satisfied that the barn was as weatherproof as it was going to get and the animals were safe and warm, Bill shut the door carefully behind him and began to walk back toward the cabin, where Ma would have a hot mug of coffee waiting for him. The sight of Prince's empty stall had blackened his mood. The sound of hoofbeats stopped him in his tracks. As always, he felt them up through the soles of his feet before he actually heard them. Perhaps Doc was coming by with the latest news. Or maybe it was Opkee. Bill scanned the horizon.

The horse was riderless. That was the first thing Bill noticed. The sight of it made him uneasy, for a riderless horse usually meant bad news. An accident, or worse. But as the horse galloped steadily closer, Bill could see it bore no saddle. The animal was running like the wind, making straight for Bill. Bill caught his breath and took a step forward, not daring to let even the beginnings of the thought into his mind. But it took only a few seconds more for the truth, the beautiful truth, to reach his eyes.

"Prince!" he shouted with all his might, running toward the horse as fast as he could go. The horse slowed to a trot, then just feet from Bill he stopped altogether, his chestnut coat glossy with sweat and steaming in the brisk air. Bill threw his arms around Prince's neck, hugging him and stroking him.

"You shook them, didn't you, clever boy!" Bill cried, trembling with the greatness of it all. "Slipped your harness and took off on those nasty border ruffians, didn't ya!"

Prince brought his head back to where Bill was standing and gave him a little nudge with his nose. Well, of course I did, the gesture said, and Bill threw back his head and laughed as he never had before.

"I shoulda known you'd do it, Prince. I shoulda known you'd find a way home to me."

He hadn't known, though. He hadn't dared hope he'd ever see his precious horse again. And here he was, a glorious Christmas present three weeks early. How wonderful it would be to burst into the cabin and give the news to his family. Julia would probably run straight out to see Prince without even putting on her shawl. And Nellie would probably squeal her sweet squeal and clap as hard as she knew how. And Ma would write to Pa straightaway and tell him, and how glad Pa would be! Pa of all people, who knew how Bill loved his horse!

He couldn't wait to tell them all. But he did wait, just one moment longer. He held on to the anticipation of good news not yet delivered. He savored the feel of Prince's mane in his hands, the hot musky smell of him, the two long lines of breath turned to smoke as the horse exhaled, the deep nickering sounds he made in his throat.

It was a strange world, and oftentimes a scary one. And today it was a cold one, too. But at this moment Bill loved the world that had shaken him up, sent him to the frontier, seen him grown before his years, and given him back his horse.

AFTERWORD

★   ★   ★

Bill Cody was a real boy, and his story is true. Years before he came to international fame as the scout and Wild West showman known as Buffalo Bill Cody, Bill and his family struggled through difficult times on the frontier. In the history books this time and place is now known as Bleeding Kansas. It marks the real beginning of the Civil War, which would erupt throughout the nation six years later. And Bill and his family not only witnessed these events, they lived them every day.

Pa really did host a Fourth of July barbecue for the Kickapoo. The invasions by the border ruffians, and Pa's escape in a long skirt and bonnet, really happened, as did Prince's abduction and his eventual return. Bill's Kickapoo friend Opkee is also a real person. Happily, as Doc Hathaway hoped, the Kickapoo tribe did win out over the hostility of some of the settlers, and the descendants of Kennekuk's people are still living on their land in Kansas today. And Isaac Cody really was stabbed at Rively's trading post by Charlie Dunn after being forced to reveal his position on the question of slavery. The newspaper account of the stabbing that Bill reads to Ma is taken word for word from an actual article.

It is difficult to imagine living in a time when the law of the land could be so casually disregarded. The acts of violence and the incidents of men voting falsely or being forced to vote against their will happened throughout Kansas Territory. As Bill learned, the North did sit up and take notice. Many began to fear that events were sliding dangerously out of control, and that it would not be long before the unrest spread beyond Kansas Territory. The issue of slavery was destined to be decided once and for all. But it would not be an easy process, and in the years to follow more would be asked of Bill—and every citizen of the nation—than anyone could ever have possibly imagined.

★ ★ ★

E. Cody Kimmel grew up hearing about the adventures of her distant relative Buffalo Bill Cody. In preparation for writing this series, she traveled the same route from Iowa to Kansas as the Codys did. Ms. Kimmel lives with her husband and daughter in New York's Hudson Valley.